Down Dog!

A Tamsin Kernick English Cozy Mystery

Book 3

Lucy Emblem

Also by the Author

More mysteries with Quiz, Banjo, and Moonbeam:

Where it all began ..

Sit, Stay, Murder!

Ready, Aim, Woof!

Down Dog!

Barks, Bikes, and Bodies!

Ma-ah, Ma-ah, Murder!

Snapped and Framed!

Christmas Carols and Canine Capers! A Howling Good Christmas Mystery!

Game, Set, and Catch!

Chapter 1

"Glad you had the time to join me today," said Tamsin. She breathed in the sharp, cool, autumnal air of the fields they were tramping through. "Unusual for us both to have an afternoon clear of clients." Though it had been dry of late, there had been a heavy dew and she was glad she'd chosen to wear wellies to wade through the wet grass.

"Yes, so am I. It's lovely. But I wish you'd told me not to wear trainers! They're sopping wet," Emerald squelched her feet around in her shoes and watched the water come bubbling out.

"That's the trouble with being a sedentary animal-lover. Always content to sit with a cat on your lap, you!"

Banjo came racing past, with Quiz and Moonbeam in hot pursuit, the little terrier Moonbeam putting on a surprising turn of speed while skilfully cutting the corners to keep up. "You see, if you had a *decent* animal, like a dog," Tamsin grinned, "you'd have to be out every day like I am."

Emerald snorted in response, but couldn't help smiling as well.

"Anyway I have to get out walking," Tamsin went on, "in order to walk off some of the calories I love to consume, specially at The Cake Stop! A surprising amount of a dog trainer's work is done sitting down, talking to the owner. It's really not fair that you can eat quantities of walnut cake or pistachio Pavlova without ever showing a bulge."

"Ah well, if you did yoga all day, as I do, you wouldn't have to worry so much about calories. It uses up an awful lot of them!" Emerald laughed and patted her friend on the back as they walked together, the tall willowy blonde girl with her rather more solid, shorter, dark-haired house-mate.

"Actually," Tamsin said, "I'm thinking of planning another mass Dog Walk. The last one got ... slightly derailed."

"That's one way of putting it!" laughed Emerald, thinking of the surprising and unwelcome events that took place that day.

"But they're such fun - and they lead to loads more bookings for me. So I'm going to get that organised soon. Might start on that tomorrow … Hey, we could walk the Worcestershire Beacon!"

They walked on together till Emerald suddenly said, "Is this where you found the blackberries the other week? That blackberry and apple crumble was *dee-lish*!"

"There was a good clump along this walk, in the hedgerow. We can have a look, but by now they may be past it."

Their walk took them through a gate where the three dogs waited patiently for permission to dive through the gap under the stile, then through a muddier wooded area, before emerging again into the sunlight and a large field which rose up before them, hinting at the steepness of the mighty Malvern Hills towering over them.

The ancient Hills - formed from the oldest rock in England - dominated the fertile landscape around Malvern, in the lush Heart of England. They changed from soft and beautiful to misty and mysterious, from bleak and exposed to resplendent and majestic. The seasons seemed to be exaggerated up in the Hills, and the weather could change from hour to hour. Wherever you were in this protected 'Area of Outstanding Natural Beauty' - one of only 30-odd in England - the Hills were visible for miles around. They felt like the guardians of this corner of England. They had been there so long, influenced so many thousands of lives. They had a permanence that inspired confidence.

The dogs were slowing down at this stage of the walk, and the women had paused to gaze up at the Hills, with a deep feeling of appreciation for their protection.

They climbed the gentle slope of their field, studying the hedgerow as Tamsin was wont to do, as she pointed out the late flowering of the bindweed and the resurgence of dandelions for one final hurrah before winter closed in.

"Here's the bramble clump .. Oh, looks as though the Pooka spat on them!"

"What?" Emerald came to get a closer look. "Oh, most of them are withered, and some have gone squishy." She sampled a couple, made a face, and said "Who spat on them?"

"The Pooka. Malevolent fairy. It's a Celtic legend. My mother would say it."

"She was a Celt?"

"Not really. A Celt by marriage, you could say! She was always in love with all things Cornish, so when she met a man whose family came from Cornwall, and had an actual Cornish name, she was smitten."

"Kernick. I wondered where it came from. And she picked up the lingo?"

"She did. Loved all the myth and magic."

"That's that then, for blackberries. The Pooka got them. Hmph!" said Emerald. Looking down at her soaking wet, mud-caked shoes she added, "Good thing we have a hose at home .. Hey! What's that?" And she bent over a clump of damp grass just by her feet, peering at the bright white shape beneath, the grass draped over it like the lattice crust on a pie.

"A mushroom!" exclaimed Tamsin happily. "I wondered if we'd find some." And she tucked her dark hair behind her ear and pulled a string bag out of her back pocket, heading towards Emerald's find. "Lovely!" she said, as she released the large mushroom from its grassy bonds, and studied the underside carefully before dropping it into her bag.

"You're not going to eat it!" Emerald looked shocked. "I was told never to eat wild mushrooms, only the ones in the shops."

"It's fine if you know what you're looking for," Tamsin replied as she picked a further three mushrooms, inspected them carefully and added them to her haul.

"And you do?" asked Emerald nervously.

"To be honest, these are the only mushrooms I can surely identify. They're Field Mushrooms. Delicious, and quite safe."

"How do you know?" Emerald still sounded doubtful.

"I've eaten hundreds of them. Look," she picked another and held it out for Emerald to look at. "See the clean white top? That means it's young and still very edible. Those over there are discolouring and a bit moth-eaten - looking old and past it."

Emerald peered at it, and peeled off some of the strands of grass adhering to it.

"Then there's the colour underneath. Rich chocolate colour of the gills." Tamsin turned the fungus over.

Emerald nodded, feeling a bit more reassured that her friend had some idea what she was doing and wasn't about to poison her.

"There's another mushroom you don't want to muddle it up with though, and that's the Yellow-Staining Mushroom. So let's test this one ..." She scored the cap of the mushroom with her fingernail, and waited.

"What are we waiting for?" Emerald peered at the mushroom.

"Yellow. If that were a Yellow-staining Mushroom it would have a smear of bright yellow round the mark by now. Also the gills tend to be pinker." Tamsin turned the mushroom over again to show the dark brown velvety gills.

Emerald held the mushroom up to her nose and sniffed cautiously. "Smells like a mushroom," she conceded.

"That's another test. If it smells mushroomy and nice, you're good to go. We can have these for supper." She smiled as she held up the string bag, now bulging with fat mushrooms.

"O-o-o-kay. But you can eat one first!"

"I'm your official taster now, am I?" Tamsin laughed, and they turned their steps towards her van beyond the next gate, the dogs now slowing down and content to walk close to them as the light started to fade. They could just see the edge of the 'Top Dogs' sign on the van through the sparse hedge.

There was a sudden flurry of activity in the tall oak trees along the field boundary, as a number of large black birds burst out and flew about cawing loudly.

"A Murder of Crows," said Tamsin, pausing to admire their beauty as they looped and dived and chased each other.

"This countryside of yours seems to be full of deadly danger!" Emerald shivered. "Malevolent fairies, poisonous mushrooms, murderous crows …"

"Actually," Tamsin said in her most matter-of-fact voice, "they're rooks, not crows."

"How on earth can you tell?"

"'A Crow in a crowd is a Rook, and a Rook on its own is a Crow.' The old sayings are often true. I guess an argument broke out up there over who was roosting on which branch."

"It's sure getting gloomy now," said Emerald nervously, speeding her steps towards the van.

"Talking of The Cake Stop as we were," said Tamsin as they continued trudging up the hill, "As we so often do," put in Emerald. "True. Well, talking of The Cake Stop, aren't you over there this evening?"

"Yep. It's my Tuesday evening class."

"Do you know, I've never been in Jean-Philippe's upper room?"

"You should come! It's nice up there. Old floorboards, and white walls with just a few framed photos of the local countryside. Just the right size for my class - there's ten students now," she added proudly.

"Didn't realise you had that many. I'll have to put the rent up!" joshed Tamsin. "Does it look out onto the street? Do you get traffic noise?"

"No, it's very quiet. The only windows look out over the courtyard behind The Cake Stop. Not a very salubrious view, but the blinds are usually down. There's a metal fire escape that leads down to the concrete area, where they have those huge bins."

"Oh yes, I know. Kylie parks her bike there before starting work. You can get to it from the alley behind the café, can't you?" They'd reached the van and Tamsin was busily drying twelve paws, while Emerald peeled off her sodden shoes and socks.

"Must do," she said, wrinkling her nose in distaste as she held the shoes out at arm's length before dropping them into the footwell. "That's where Kylie must get in. And the bin men have to get their truck along there. I only use the front door and go up the stairs at the back of the café. You wouldn't know the room was there if .. if you didn't know!"

"Sounds a bit Irish to me! But no, you can't see it from the main part of the café, can you. Your secret hideaway!"

"It works well. They can arrive a bit early and have a coffee before we start class. Then it becomes a regular meeting-place for them, so Jean-Philippe is happy with the extra custom. To be honest, he doesn't charge much for the room."

"He's a good egg, is Jean-Philippe. Or perhaps I should say, *un bon oeuf*."

"Idiot!" laughed Emerald, "or should I say *imbécile*?"

Chapter 2

"You know what?" said Tamsin as they arrived home. "I'll settle the dogs while you get ready, and I'll come up to The Cake Stop with you. I'm at a loose end this evening - my one appointment got cancelled. Flu. Though that will give me some time to work on my monthly piece for the *Malvern Mercury* when I get home."

"*Tamsin's DoggyTails?*"

"Haha. No, just *Your Dog in October. Ask the Dog Trainer* is its official name," she said with pride. "It's actually doing well - I get quite a few enquiries from it," she smiled.

"Sure, we can walk up together." Emerald took her shoes out to the back to hose them straight away.

"I can meet some of your students!" Tamsin called out to her through the open door.

"And you can eat cake. I know," laughed Emerald. "Oh hello Opal, you don't want to get near me at the moment - you'll get splashed, and you know how cats hate getting wet!" Opal put one paw in the growing puddle by the tap, hastily removing it, giving it a distasteful shake before walking back into the house, tail up like a flag.

So once they were ready, they set off again, this time on foot.

"I've done enough walking today to warrant cream in my coffee as well as cake," Tamsin smiled as they walked, Emerald with her yoga mat bag slung over her shoulder, something she'd picked up on a trip to Bali. And they enjoyed their stroll across the Common and along the top road to Great Malvern as the sky darkened and the ornate old gaslights switched themselves on.

"These old gas lamps are amazing," said Emerald as she admired the soft glow from the old-fashioned lantern above her.

"They are. But actually that is one of the electric imitations. Most of the real ones are back along the top road."

Emerald tilted her head. "But I can hear it hissing!"

"Very authentic, aren't they!"

"You're having me on! I'm not sure I believe you. How do you know all this?"

"It's true, really. I was walking along past the real gas lamps one day and there was a guy up a ladder fiddling with one of them. We got talking. Enthusiasts are always keen to teach."

"That's what we are - enthusiasts."

"And it's why we're so good at what we do!" grinned Tamsin, as she pushed open the big wooden and glass door of their favourite café.

Kylie, the trainee barista, tossed her pink hair out of her eyes and gave them a beaming smile as they arrived in The Cake Stop. "Let me see, she said, that's a Flat White for you Emerald, and a Cappuccino for you Tamsin?"

"Got it in one," smiled Tamsin and started studying the gorgeous cakes in the display cabinet. "Furies been busy?"

"Damaris was in this morning with that almond and syrup cake, the one with the flaked almonds all round the sides?"

"They really do have great ideas," said Tamsin, her mouth watering already, and thinking of the remarkable three elderly sisters - known by all as The Furies because of their Greek mythology names - who ran the little catering company Dodds & Co.

"Well I'll have a go at that one! What about you, Emerald?"

"Not before class I'm afraid! I wouldn't be able to bend."

"You can have some of mine - you have to at least taste it."

So they headed over to a group of tables on the far side of the café, already occupied by a very erect elderly lady talking to a past pupil of Tamsin's.

"Hi Shirley!" Tamsin greeted her ex-student. "Good to see you - how's Luke?"

"Oh, hallo Tamsin. I forgot you knew Emerald. Yes, Luke's fine thanks - not getting any smaller," she gave a tense smile, as she referred to her very large but friendly Pyrenean Mountain Dog.

"And this is Linda," said Emerald, indicating the straight-backed and very slender lady seated beside Shirley, her grey hair swept up into a bun on the top of her head, ballerina-style.

Exchanging greetings, they all settled themselves with their drinks. Tamsin felt a bit of a pig eating cake while no-one else did, but she was so hungry after her exertions that she dug in all the same.

"So how long have you been coming to this class?" she asked Linda.

"Oh, a long time now. Emerald is so good! I used to be a ballet dancer, you see, and I don't feel right if I'm not keeping myself physically fit."

"I bet you can do things now that I've *never* been able to do!" laughed Tamsin. "I bet you can do the splits!"

"I can," Linda smiled back, "and I plan on being able to do them when I'm 107, like that remarkable cricketer woman who died recently."

Tamsin was interrupted in her munching from time to time by new people joining the group, all carrying yoga mats and towels. She met a young woman called Saffron, who kept checking her phone. "New baby," whispered Emerald.

"Ooh sorry," said Saffron - just want to make sure I told her where Fuzzy Bear is," and she tapped out yet another message to her long-suffering baby-sitter.

"How old is your baby?" Tamsin enquired politely, knowing this would be the only subject Saffron would want to talk about.

"He's twelve weeks," said Saffron with a rapt, angelic, expression. "I hate leaving him, but I had to do something about this," and she patted her tummy, which looked pretty flat to Tamsin, whose tummy was now full of cake.

"It's Tamsin, Mummy!" a young voice piped up behind her, and she turned to see Molly and young Cameron.

"So you come here too!" she said, smiling broadly at Molly and her little boy.

"Just when Chas's work and school events allow."

"You too, Cameron?" And as the boy nodded vigorously she said, "I bet you're super-bendy, with all that running around with Buster."

"He is," interjected Linda. "I'd love to see him take up dancing."

Cameron pulled a face befitting a nine-year-old boy who's had ballet dancing suggested to him, remembered his manners and smiled back at Linda, who confided, "We ballerinas wouldn't get far without the strong men to lift us."

A minor commotion at the door distracted them as a flustered young man tried to hold the door open for some departing customers, and managed only to drop his mat and towel and scatter his bag of papers all over the floor, as the customers darted through the door before it closed on them.

"Ah, Harry," sighed Emerald, getting up to go and help him. And as they gathered up his belongings, a large man who, despite the cold, was wearing a sleeveless tank top which exposed his very well-muscled arms - walked straight past them without a word and headed towards the stairs at the back of the shop, a yoga mat peeping out from his bag.

"Typical Harry," said Molly, now seated in Emerald's place. "Nice enough, but scatterbrained," she sighed.

"And typical Kurt," said Linda sniffily. Seeing Tamsin's questioning look she added quietly, "Keeps himself to himself," as she nodded to the big man by the stairs.

"Any good at yoga?"

"Oh yes, he can do all the tough poses. Very strong," she nodded, approvingly.

Tamsin noticed they'd been joined at the end of the table by a young redheaded man, who was keenly chatting to Saffron. Following her gaze, Molly said, "That's Andrew. Nice young fellow - puts me to shame with what he can do! He's missing Sara, I think."

"Sara?"

"Yes, you must know her - that business in Bishop's Green in the summer?"

"Oh yes, that Sara! But isn't she at college now?"

"I believe so. But Andrew lives in hope she might be back home for a few days and will appear here. So he's making do with Saffron meanwhile."

"It's a bit off her patch - does she have a car?"

"She gets a lift with Julia. Do you know her? She's always talking about her dog, so perhaps you do?"

"Romeo? Sure I know him - and her! Fancy that ..." and Tamsin ate the last spoonful of almond cake, thinking back to when she'd first arrived in this town, not knowing a soul.

A twittering caused Tamsin to turn round again, as in the open doorway she saw two shapeless middle-aged women volubly saying goodbye to someone. She peered past the reflections on the window and saw her friend Charity leading her little dog Muffin away. And as the two women arrived at the table, still chattering, Molly introduced them as Jane and Alice, stalwarts of the yoga group.

"Oh, we're not very good," giggled Jane, and Alice leant over and joined in, "No good at all really, but we do like to *try!*"

"You know Charity?" It was one of those moments when the room you're pitching your voice over suddenly goes quiet. And was filled with a chorus of Yeses.

"That's nearly all of you!" laughed Tamsin.

Emerald, who'd arrived back with the flustered Harry - now trying to fit himself and his baggage in at the table with many 'excuse me's' and 'forgive me's' - said, "You should know - everyone knows Charity!"

"Small world, this," smiled Tamsin. And as Jane and Alice both cornered Emerald with cries of "Tell us about that Yoga Retreat you're going to, Emerald!" "Isn't it very soon?" Tamsin noticed an attractive girl with striking long dark glossy wavy hair who'd joined them quietly. Her skin was pasty beneath the olive colour, her eyes were cast down and she had no drink.

"Yes, it's next weekend ... You ok, Gabrielle?" asked Emerald turning to her with concern.

"Just feeling a bit odd. Maybe I've got something coming on," she mumbled. "Can't face a coffee at the moment."

"Are you sure you should be here? Wouldn't you be better off in bed?"

"Oh no, I'd hate to miss class," Gabrielle smiled wanly. "I'll be fine with a bit of movement. I've been standing around in the shop all day."

"If you don't feel up to it, be sure to tell me," nodded Emerald.

Gabrielle didn't look at all 'fine' to Tamsin, but then she didn't know how she usually looked. "Say, don't you work in the health shop?" She suddenly remembered having seen her before, when she was deliberating between a large and confusing array of dried beans, and Gabrielle had helped her choose.

"Yes I do! Not a very good advertisement for them at the moment, I'm afraid," she said shyly.

"Perhaps you've eaten something that doesn't agree with you, dear?" said Jane.

"You do look a bit green round the gills," added Alice with concern.

"Think you should see a doctor?"

Gabrielle held up her hands, "Oh no, no doctor, thank you! I don't do doctors," and attempted a smile.

"Time to get started," said Emerald brightly, before the two ladies could make Gabrielle feel worse, and with a great scraping of chairs and pushing of tables, they all rose, claimed their various yoga mats and towels and bags, and formed a loose crocodile towards the stairs, where Kurt was still waiting in silence.

"Enjoy your class!" Tamsin called and sat back in her chair as Kylie approached with a large tray and her ever-present tea towel draped over her shoulder.

"That's a motley crew," said Tamsin, as Kylie adjusted her tiny mini-skirt before bending over the table and starting to stack all the crockery on her tray. Tamsin passed over her plate and mug.

"That's one way of saying it!" agreed Kylie enthusiastically, her pink hair flopping over her eyes till she tossed it back again. "Never seen such a bunch of different people all with the same interest. They're here every week, you know."

"I expect they come back at other times to sample the food on offer?" asked Tamsin with a wink.

"Oh yes. Once teacher isn't there they'll all happily plough through the cakes!" She grinned.

And so, having had a glimpse into Emerald's world, and thinking about her own 'motley crew' of students at her various classes, all united by a love of their dog or perhaps a frustration with their dog, Tamsin checked her pockets for her phone and keys and, waving a cheery goodbye to Kylie, she set off home. She passed Jean-Philippe near the door and greeted him cheerily, "Hi Jean-Philippe!"

"*Salut!*" he said with a broad smile, and turned back to carry on chatting to his new customers.

Tamsin sighed with pleasure as she left the thriving little café. She loved this place, this town, and all her friends and acquaintances in it. "What did they put in that Almond Cake?" she laughed to herself and strode down the hill, keen to get started on her new piece for the paper.

Chapter 3

News travels fast in a small town. And the next morning, while Tamsin was making an early morning cuppa and getting ready to leave for her first home visit of several that day - to a family terrorised by their biting puppy - she could hear the sound of wind chimes that signalled Emerald's phone ringing upstairs, followed by anxious talking. Before she could make out what was being said, her own phone rang - with a heavy rock number of Bryan Adams - and she found Charity shouting in her ear.

"My dear, you won't believe what's happened!" she said excitedly, "No Muffin, leave Sapphire's tail alone ..."

"What?" demanded Tamsin impatiently. "What's happened?"

"I'm surprised Emerald hasn't told you .. *Muffin!*"

"Told me what?" said Tamsin, feeling exasperated.

"About the dead body."

"Dead body?"

"Is the line poor? I said, *the dead body.*" Charity enunciated clearly.

"Charity! I can hear you fine - just tell me." It was time for her class-mistress tone.

"Oh well, you see, I was passing The Cake Stop this morning. I was going to see if they had any more of my wool in the knitting shop - I'm nearly out, and I need another ball of the orange .."

"Charity!"

"Oh yes. And there was police tape all round the café. And down the alley at the side. I went to peep and that nice Sergeant shooed me away. But not before I'd seen the ambulance people zipping up a bag and placing it gently onto a stretcher."

"No! Who? *Who is it*, Charity?"

"They wouldn't say."

"But - Jean-Philippe? Kylie?" Tamsin shouted, the strain clear in her voice.

"Oh, they're fine. They were both talking to one of the policemen."

Tamsin reached out for a chair and slumped into it with relief. Instantly two canine chins arrived on her thigh, and four little canine paws landed lightly in her lap. "You know, don't you, guys?"

"What's that, dear? Know who?"

"Sorry Charity, I was just surprised that the dogs knew I needed support."

"Oh dogs always know, Muffin hasn't left my side since we came home."

"Charity, I must talk to Emerald - I believe she's just learning the same news. Talk later, bye!"

And as she slipped her phone back in her pocket she heard Emerald coming down the stairs, not in her usual floaty goddess-like way, but harum-scarum and hurried, Opal bounding down the stairs behind her.

"Have you heard?" Emerald gasped. "It's Gabrielle! Gabrielle's dead!" and she put her hands to her head and started to whimper.

"Sit down," ordered Tamsin. "I've got to go out soon, but there's time for a soothing cup of tea and some toast." And she headed for the kettle.

"Oh no, no toast! It's too ghastly!"

"Who was that on the phone?"

"It was Jean-Philippe. It seems Kylie arrived this morning and came through the courtyard to chain up her bike, and she found .. she found this body splayed out on the concrete. Oh, it's horrible ..."

"Here, get yourself outside this." Tamsin handed her a mug of tea, steaming in the chilly October morning.

Emerald clutched it and drank. And the colour began to return to her pale cheeks. Opal was purring on her lap, not even demanding her breakfast as she normally did.

"They know, you know," said Tamsin, nodding at Opal.

"I wish they knew what had happened." She stroked Opal's back heavily. "I feel terrible. She was a student in *my* class. How on earth did she end up dead?" And she started to cry in earnest.

It took a while for Tamsin to calm Emerald sufficiently to be able to face even a bit of the world. Eventually Emerald was able to stop crying and take some deep breaths. She went upstairs again, cuddling Opal closely to her, to wash her face with cool water.

"Look, I have to get off in a minute .." Tamsin called up the stairs as she packed her home visit bag and got together the details of her new client and their nipping puppy. "What are you going to do?"

"I have to go to The Cake Stop!" she called back, as she arrived at the top of the stairs and started a more usual goddess-like floaty descent, her cat padding down in front of her, dot-dot-dot.

"I'll drop you there on my way," said Tamsin decisively, grabbing her keys. "Come on, let's go!"

And after settling the dogs - who wouldn't be coming this morning - they headed out to the van.

"I'm so used to walking across the Common, I'd forgotten this road entirely," said Emerald, making a great effort to resume her usual calm state.

"Yes, it's always so dark, with the Hills rising up steeply just beside us."

"Aren't you planning your next big dog walk up on the Hills?"

"Yeah, I must get it organised before it gets too cold up there!"

"I'd been thinking of a yoga outing ..."

"What a lovely idea! Why don't we combine forces?" said Tamsin with pleasure. "We can have a Dog and Yoga outing - you've already got some of my students in your classes anyway, I see!"

"I like that. Yes - that would be fun!"

"Cheer up girl," said Tamsin, putting a hand on Emerald's arm as she pulled up outside the blue and white striped police-tape-bedecked Cake Stop. "Whatever happened cannot possibly be considered your fault."

"Now I know how you felt over that Nether Trotley business, Tamsin. Who's going to want to come to a yoga class where you end up dead?"

"Look, over there, past all the gawpers, I can see Jean-Philippe talking to that nice police sergeant. Go and join him - he'll see you right."

"Thanks Tamsin - you'd better hurry or you'll be late to your session. I'll see you back home later. Leave your phone on - I'll let you know of any developments. I don't even know what family Gabrielle had ... Jean-Philippe said he'd rung the health shop ..."

"Go!" said Tamsin firmly, and put the van in gear again. "You'll be fine. See you later," and she drove off down the hill towards Worcester, wondering how yet again she was tangled up in a violent death.

Chapter 4

After four different home visits back to back, three close together in the Worcester direction and the last on the Gloucester road, Tamsin was worn out as she drove home. But she went the long way round specially so she could pass The Cake Stop, and she saw that the tape had gone and the café was open and apparently back to normal.

"That was quick," she said to the dogs in the back of the van, before she remembered that they were still at home. "I'm going batty," she said slowly, blushing slightly, as she turned the van towards Pippin Lane.

She was too tired right now to visit the café, and realised she'd be on duty Emerald-minding as soon as she got home. This poor girl was known to her! She'd been in her classes for some time. This was so much worse for Emerald than it had been for Tamsin on the previous occasions when she'd had a close brush with sudden death.

So she was glad - after greeting all the dogs, who were insistent on leading her to the living room - to find her friend stretched out on the sofa, Opal parked on her chest purring. Tamsin perched on the arm of the sofa while Quiz and Banjo sniffed Emerald's face, checking just how she was, and Moonbeam hopped up and curled up in the dent of the cushion beside her. Clearly she'd been busy tending to Emerald already!

Emerald looked pale and drawn, deflated where she was normally so full of vibrant energy. "You're right, they do know."

"Yes, and I know too. Have you eaten today?"

Emerald slowly shook her head from side to side.

"I'm going to remedy that right away - 'but me no buts'!" Tamsin said quickly, raising a finger as she saw Emerald thinking of saying no. And she went to the kitchen, to return a short while later with two mugs of hot chocolate, and a couple of cheese toasties.

"I didn't have time for lunch either," she said as she chomped hungrily into her sandwich. "And you're not going to say a word till you've got all this down you."

Emerald could see when she was beaten, and smiled shyly as she pulled herself upright, Opal leaping off her chest and stalking away to the cat flap, tail held high. And from a gingerish start Emerald clearly found that she *was* hungry after all, and made short work of the meal.

"Thanks, I do feel a little better," she said.

"Great! Now - give me all the news!"

Emerald stayed sitting up while she said, "Honestly, there isn't much. Kylie made the awful discovery this morning when she arrived at about quarter to ten to open up. She could see straight away that Gabrielle was dead - she recognised her, of course - and she was just calling the police when Jean-Philippe arrived through the front of the shop. There's no gate onto the alley at the back, so they had to stay there to guard the place till the police arrived. Kylie was in quite a state."

"I can imagine," said Tamsin.

".. But she had to stay there. As soon as the boys in blue arrived, Jean-Philippe sent her into the café to sit down, so he could handle the police. Then of course, the ambulance men turned up."

"Loadsa questions, I suppose?"

"Loadsa questions. It was a good hour before the police were finished and Gabrielle was taken away." Emerald screwed up her eyes, took a deep breath, and carried on.

"How long was the café closed?"

"Most of the day, I believe. The courtyard was placed out of bounds, and that's still got blue and white tape all over the place. Kylie told me they had to park all their rubbish on the stairs to take it home with them. No access to the bins."

"But I don't suppose there was much rubbish, as they were closed for half the day?"

"You'd be surprised! That crowd that was outside - as soon as they were allowed they all flooded in."

"Ghouls!"

"Yes, they are. But I guess that's human nature."

"How long did you stay?"

"Several hours, on and off. The police had loads of questions for me too. But honestly," she looked appealingly at Tamsin, "I couldn't tell them much!"

"So what *did* you tell them?"

"I don't remember last night all that clearly, didn't think it important at the time. How wrong I was!"

Tamsin waited quietly, while Emerald sat forward on the sofa and said, "You see, Gabrielle really wasn't doing too well. I suggested several times that she should go home, but she wanted to stay. She was skipping all the poses that needed her head to be lower than her hips."

"That's most of them from the little yoga I know!"

"Yes, quite a lot of them are. But she was managing the floor moves. Anyway, at some stage - I believe it was just before we finished, just before the Savasana - she said something about needing some fresh air, and she went out onto the fire escape. There's a curtain over the door and the window beside it, and the door kinda got pushed to. So I was clearing everything up, and chatting and seeing everyone off and - you know how it goes. I collected up all the tea lights and swept up the ash from under the joss stick, made sure everything was done .. and I turned out the lights and shut the door behind me. Tamsin, it's awful!" Emerald turned moist eyes to her, "I forgot Gabrielle! I didn't notice! I didn't notice the fire door wasn't completely shut, and I forgot!"

She started to whimper again, and Tamsin hopped over to sit next to her and put an arm round her shoulder.

"I don't know how long she was out there, or why!"

"But she wasn't shut out? And she could always have gone down the fire escape if she had been? You're not to blame, Emerald!"

"That's true, she could have gone down the stairs. But maybe she fainted! They found some vomit out there, on the railings and on the concrete, apparently. She was out there being ill and no-one noticed! I feel so bad!" She blew her nose loudly then said, "You see I checked the room before I left. I always do. To make sure it's all neat and tidy and nothing's been left behind. There was nothing there. Nothing! She must have taken her yoga bag out with her."

"Maybe she thought she'd make a quick getaway - not have to talk to anyone if she was feeling so ill."

"Maybe. But I feel so bad that I didn't notice her when we were leaving."

In an attempt to stop the tears flowing again, Tamsin said sharply, "So do they think she fainted and fell? Or was leaning over to throw up and tipped over?"

"They won't say. They were taking all sorts of measurements apparently, and Jean-Philippe said they took loads of photos too. They may know more when the post mortem is done,"

"The post mortem! Of course! I'll get on to Maggie in a moment and see if she's free for a walk tomorrow - I'm free in the morning. Do you want to stretch a leg in a delightful orchard? I'm sure it would do you good."

"Okay. I'm free in the morning too. Let's hope Maggie is. Pretty handy, you being friends with the police pathologist!"

"We get to meet a lot of interesting people through our classes, don't we! You had a good few interesting people in your class last night ... I wonder ..."

"Oh no, Tamsin! You don't think one of the others is implicated? Surely not! I know you have a nose for this, but it seems like an accident? Just an accident?"

"It would be good - though tragic, of course - if it were. But my spidey senses tell me that something's off. They're tingling! I'm going to ring Maggie now," and she rose purposefully, picked up the cups and plates and headed for the phone.

"Got to check my enquiries anyway. Here, have a cat," and with her free hand she scooped up Opal who had just returned to the room, and tossed her onto Emerald's lap, as all the dogs got up and followed her out to the kitchen.

Tamsin went through all her enquiries first. Whatever was happening, she had to keep her business going! And finishing up her last call with "I really look forward to meeting you and your dog, Sandra! Just get that enrolment completed tonight to ensure your place is held. See you soon!" she noticed Emerald's phone flashing on the worktop nearby.

She took it into the living room. "I'm just going to ring Maggie. Looks as though you've got a thousand messages here," and she handed her the phone. "Coffee?"

"Thanks, yes please. I'm feeling a tiny bit better. Let's see these messages …"

And while the kettle boiled, Tamsin gave Maggie a buzz.

"Thought I might be hearing from you!" Maggie smiled. "You know I can't tell you anything … yet?"

"I know! But you can imagine - Emerald's in bits. You're not free for a walk with Jez tomorrow morning, are you?"

"Yes, if you're early enough. Orchard ok?"

"Perfect! Emerald wants to come. She needs to get out into the fresh air and clear her head. That ok?"

"Of course, we can enjoy kicking through the leaves. It's getting a bit muddy underfoot there, what with all the machinery they've had working up and down the rows. But it's still lovely!"

They fixed a time and Tamsin took the coffee mugs into the living room. "All fixed for tomorrow morning. This time you absolutely need wellies, ok?"

"I won't be caught out again! I've had loads of messages from people. Some are from last night's students - they've just heard about it. And a couple from other students who don't even come to The Cake Stop classes who are worried they'll die on their mats."

"Some people are just worriers. I remember from the Nether Trotley affair ... but look how well that class is doing now! It even has a waiting list."

"That's true. I just texted them that I'd tell them more when I know more. Can't do much else." Her phone pinged again and she glanced down at it in her hand. "Oh, Feargal! Let's see what he has to say."

Feargal, the *Malvern Mercury* reporter who had become their friend over the last few months, had left a message, Emerald's phone having been on silent all day. "He's really worried about us. Better get back to him."

"I'm sure he's more worried about you," said Tamsin meaningfully.

Emerald blushed slightly and started tapping out a message. "You know," she said, as she finished, "I'm really tired. I'm going to turn in early tonight and be fresh for tomorrow morning's walk."

"I have no more work today. We can wrap ourselves in duvets and watch a film - something light or funny - what do you think?"

"You're right. 'Sufficient unto the day is the evil thereof,' as my Granny used to enjoy saying, when she'd cleared away dinner and sat down with her embroidery."

"That's a good idea - not embroidery! - but you can help me making these tug toys for class. That'll keep us amused!" And she reached for her big bag of fleece fabric while Emerald flicked through the tv channels to find them something innocuous to distract them.

And by mutual agreement they stopped all discussion of Gabrielle's demise, and escaped from reality for a few blissful hours, into a silly rom-com.

Chapter 5

Tamsin and Emerald drove along the narrow back roads of Herefordshire - one of the most sparsely populated of the English counties - admiring the misty fields they could see through the now-bare hedges. The three friends arrived on time at the orchard, out towards Bingham Parva where Maggie lived in a beautiful stone house next to the canal. Tamsin had brought all the dogs so Emerald could handle little Moonbeam and feel gainfully employed, not a passenger. They were well wrapped up against the Autumn chill, the early morning mist beginning to lift as they began their walk.

And for quite some time they were absorbed in watching the joy of the four dogs as they gambolled through the fallen leaves, or ran, or snuffled, depending on their inclination. Quiz and Jez were happy to mooch along together, while Banjo - the anxious one - was more comfortable staying safely the far side of Tamsin. Moonbeam did her usual trick of racing about round everyone, through the bigger dogs' legs, under their bellies, full of joy and energy.

"I see why you do this," said Emerald, enjoying the show.

"Couldn't do without it!" said Tamsin.

"It's something I'm just getting used to," Maggie said. "Jez is our first dog - he's a great success, bless him!"

"It's fortunate you can juggle your work-hours as you do."

"There isn't enough unexplained death around these parts to keep me busy full-time I'm happy to say, so that means I can do my consulting as well as a bit of teaching at the University. And even as a frantically busy GP, Don does get some time off too."

"There seems to *me* to be an awful lot of unexplained death round here," Emerald shuddered.

"Not really - it's just that you keep getting involved in it!" Maggie grinned.

"Not by choice!" Emerald assured her. "It's usually Tamsin who kicks it off."

Tamsin smiled. "Just a knack I have ..."

"I did the PM yesterday." When Maggie said this, they all stopped dead in their tracks.

"And?" Tamsin probed.

"And that poor girl had so much poison in her system she'd have been dead anyway in a few days."

Tamsin and Emerald gasped out together, *"Poison?"*

"Slow-acting. She'd have lived - in great pain - for a few more days."

"What was the poison?"

"Amanitin. It's found in the Death Cap Mushroom. It's deadly if not treated immediately." Maggie started walking again as she continued explaining to her aghast and silent audience. "It goes through phases. First you feel sick and giddy as your blood pressure plummets. It seems that's the stage Gabrielle was at. Then you get a few days' respite and you think it's all over."

"But it's not?" asked Emerald tremulously.

"No. After three to six days your liver packs up. It's curtains for you, to use a much-loved medical term."

"So ... she was going to die anyway?"

"Without urgent early hospital intervention, yes. And it seems she hadn't alerted a doctor at all. The police checked already."

"And she felt so ill she tumbled off the fire escape?" asked Emerald hopefully.

"This is a tough one. Since you're both so closely involved I'm going to give you a little more info. This is all strictly confidential, right?"

"Right." They intoned together, as Moonbeam raced back from one of her forays into the undergrowth, barked once with excitement, and scooted off again.

"It'll come out at the inquest, but the police may want it kept quiet till then. Naturally she had a head injury and a lot of bruising and internal damage commensurate with a fall onto a hard surface. But she landed on her front. There was also a firm red mark between her shoulder blades. She had her yoga bag slung round her, and the buckle on the strap made a clear indentation."

"She was pushed?"

"It's highly possible."

"So someone wanted her dead and didn't know she was already dying?" said sweet Emerald.

"Or someone wanted to be sure to finish the job they'd started," Tamsin said grimly.

They walked on a few steps in silence.

"Remember to keep this under your hat!" warned Maggie, "or Chief Inspector Hawkins will have my guts for garters."

"Another medical term?" smiled Tamsin. "We will. But my goodness, this puts a different complexion on it!"

"There's another thing," Maggie added. "There's clear bruising of a hand gripping her left ankle."

"Her ankle?"

"Lift and push, looks like."

"That's ghastly …"

"You can get fingerprints?" Emerald gaped at her.

"No, but the size of the hand may help to narrow down suspects in the end."

"Good heavens, that's amazing!" Tamsin spoke with awe.

"But who on earth could have wanted to kill her - twice!" Emerald looked stricken.

"You see, I told you it wasn't your fault! It was nothing to do with you. Where you *can* help is racking your brains for who else may have gone out through that fire escape door."

"I didn't see anyone go out there. But the room isn't locked. Anyone could go up the stairs from inside the café - though it's long closed by the time we finish. I make sure the front door closes and locks behind me."

They all paused, and thought over this new riddle, as a cacophony of cawing broke out in the tall trees bordering the orchard.

"There's your Murder of Crows again, Tamsin," said Emerald gloomily.

"They're following us about. ... but anyone could have gone up the fire escape from the courtyard! There's no gate from the alley," said Tamsin in a flash of comprehension.

"At least that puts the other students out of the frame," Emerald said with relief.

"Not so fast!" the ever-practical Maggie put in. "Gabrielle may have fainted, or sat down to get over her dizziness. She could have been there for some time before she went over the edge. We can only give a rough estimate of the time of death."

"So anyone could have done it?"

"Anyone."

Tamsin picked up a small bendy stick and tossed it away from the dogs, so that those who wanted to could fetch it. Banjo trotted back with the prize. A couple more throws and she said, "How on earth did she get mushroom poisoning?"

Emerald said, "She worked in the health shop. Maybe she's into foraging - oh, I'm so glad you knew what you were doing when you gathered those Field Mushrooms for us! Do these Death thingies even grow round here?"

"I'm glad you can recognise Field Mushrooms, Tamsin. Stick with what you know! And yes, Death Caps are commonly found all over the world. Easy enough to find, if you know what you're looking for."

"She could have just picked them herself - eaten the wrong mushrooms ..."

"Or someone could have fed them to her, on purpose," said Tamsin firmly. "It's a bit of a coincidence that she may have been pushed to her death the same day she'd taken enough poison to kill her. How much would that be, by the way?"

"As little as an ounce - twenty grams or so," replied Maggie.

"So just a sliver of mushroom? That could easily be concealed in - almost any dish!"

"But if it were cooked, would it still kill you?" asked Emerald.

"Oh yes. Cooking doesn't affect the strength of the poison."

"We're dealing with a monster," Tamsin frowned.

"I'm afraid we are. But the big question is 'why'? Why would anyone want to kill Gabrielle?"

"She was nice," said Emerald quietly. "Straightforward, I thought her. Nothing odd … The others liked her too. Andrew enjoyed chatting to her about South America - he's into travel." She peered at a distant hill, now emerging from the mists. "Harry was always hanging round her."

"Did Gabrielle go in for natural remedies?"

"I think so - I remember her mentioning Feverfew once, when Saffron had a headache and didn't want to take any headache pills because of her pregnancy."

"Maybe she was into making remedies too? Maybe she took something like that instead of going to the hospital. Mind you - if she didn't know she'd eaten any mushrooms, she would have just assumed it was a tummy bug."

"I do remember her mentioning a brother once. Gloucester direction? Maybe he'd know more."

"This is where Feargal could help us .."

"But you're not going to tell the press what I've told you," Maggie fixed Tamsin with a stare.

"No no, really, we won't. We can just ask him to get some background - perhaps that Emerald would like to talk to whoever was her closest relative or something. These journalists are always dredging up people's history - they know all the tricks!"

"I can see I've put up a hare for you," Maggie smiled.

"It's a good one! But I was already drawn in. Emerald's reputation is at stake here."

"Good thing she shares a house with The Malvern Hills Detective!" Maggie teased gently.

Tamsin watched Quiz and Banjo trotting along ahead of them, as Jez had fallen in beside Maggie. Tucking some stray hairs back under her woolly hat, she said, "Let's enjoy this glorious Autumn walk for a little longer. We can all get back to these grim realities as soon as we leave."

And they breathed in the fresh cool air, and walked through the damp long grass and the crunchy leaves, Emerald beginning to kick her boots through it like a small child, leaning into the healing power of nature and the countryside.

Chapter 6

When they'd got back and had lunch, Tamsin's phone rang. She'd missed several calls from Feargal while out on their walk, so she guessed it would be him ringing now.

"Are you alright?" he almost shouted. "I've been trying to get you for ages, and Emerald's not picking up either," he raced on breathlessly, raising his voice above traffic noise. He was clearly walking fast down a busy street.

"Emerald's recovering from her shock, and she doesn't need endless ghoulish enquiries, so we decided to leave her phone off. It never stopped beeping and ringing yesterday. But we're fine!"

"Well, that's a relief. I've been worried about you."

"Hmm, don't remember you getting worried about *me* before ..." Tamsin teased.

"You two are a liability. I can't turn my back without you tripping over yet another corpse. What's going on? I bet you're up to your neck investigating - I know you, Ms Kernick!"

"It's hard when the bodies hurl themselves at my feet. But seriously, we're looking at Emerald's livelihood. We have to clear this up."

"Clear what up? An accidental fall?" prodded Feargal, his journo nose twitching.

"Let's just say I'm curious," said Tamsin, keeping Maggie's instruction in mind.

"Yeah, right. You know something. Council of war?"

"Ok. We're here now - that do?"

"I'll be there in a moment - just time for you to get the cafetiere ready." Tamsin could picture his impish grin as he rang off.

And sure enough, it wasn't more than ten minutes before the sleeping dogs leapt up at the sound of his car pulling up in Pippin Lane and Feargal appeared at the door - getting the usual excited welcome from Quiz and Moonbeam, while shy Banjo stayed back a little, his tail flipping gently from side to side as he recognised their friend and gingerly sniffed his knee as they all got a friendly greeting.

"So the fact is," concluded Tamsin as they sat themselves in her living room cradling their mugs of coffee to keep warm as the October day cooled fast, "that it seems odd to me that if Gabrielle felt unwell she should have fallen over the top of the fire escape hand-rail. I could believe that she could tumble down the stairs. But she didn't. She went over the barrier and straight down. Maximum impact." She sat back and congratulated herself on voicing her suspicions without having breached Maggie's trust.

"So you reckon she was helped over?"

"At the very least. It doesn't make sense otherwise. She must have been feeling weak - and that rail is quite high. Just leaning over to throw up wouldn't work. Unless she were hugely tall - but she wasn't."

"About the same height as you, Tamsin," said Emerald. "But even I wouldn't fall over by leaning over, I don't think, and I'm a lot taller." She noticed Feargal gazing appreciatively at her long legs, and tucked them up under her.

"And who would have had access to her?" asked Feargal, as ever twitchy and fidgeting with energy.

"I think the question should be 'who would have known she was there'?" said Tamsin, as Feargal looked at her quizzically. "Emerald saw no-one go out onto the fire escape from the upper room after Gabrielle went to get some fresh air .."

"And I've been going over and over it, and I'm sure everyone else came down the stairs with me or had gone down before I closed the door," Emerald interjected.

"So I reckon someone came up the fire escape to her." Feargal nodded slowly as Tamsin spoke, and he said, "someone who knew she was there."

"Exactly! The alley leads to the service areas at the back of the other buildings too. But it stretches the imagination that a random stranger came by, saw Gabrielle and decided to climb the stairs and throw her over the top."

"This area - it would have been dark at the end of your class, yes?" Feargal asked Emerald, who was looking upset again.

"Oh yes. Dark long since."

"But apparently there's a security light out there, a motion sensor, you know?" Tamsin leant forward with her coffee. "And Jean-Philippe told Emerald it's deserted at night. It's easy enough to leave the front of The Cake Stop, head off down the road, then double back and slip into the alley. Have you been there?"

"Is the Pope a Catholic?" Feargal raised an eyebrow.

"Of course you have!" Tamsin smiled admiringly. "So you've seen the lie of the land."

"I was there in the daylight. Presumably if someone came into the area at night, the security light would go on?"

"I don't know. Maybe it points to the back door of the café, so that someone bringing rubbish out to those big bins can see. It probably was never considered necessary to light the access from the alley."

"So it may not have turned on at all?" asked Emerald quietly, now cuddling the purring Opal.

"No. Maybe not. That's something we can find out from Jean-Philippe or Kylie easily enough."

Feargal nodded, and jotted a few words into his notebook.

"And if she was feeling really faint, she may not have seen them coming up the fire escape?"

"In my experience, those sort of metal stairs are pretty noisy. They clang as you walk on them. She must have been upright," Tamsin paused to consider her words without giving anything away, "I mean not sitting down with her head in her hands, to have fallen over. So presumably she would have seen her visitor."

"Maybe they offered to help her down, so she stood up!" Emerald called out, her voice muffled by Opal's plentiful cream fur as the cat smarmed her face. The others nodded as they considered this.

"Either way, we don't know if they were known to her. I mean, if she felt really ill, she would have done what they said, wouldn't she."

"I agree, a random stranger seems unlikely. It's not as if - from what you say - she was in a fit enough state to be able to fight them if they were trying it on," said Feargal pensively.

"So we're looking at someone who knew she was there, and who wanted her dead," said Tamsin. "Ok, Emerald, so which of your students wanted her out of the way?"

Emerald gasped and her mouth stayed open as she clutched Opal closer to her.

"I mean, who else would have known?" Tamsin spread her hands out and lifted her shoulders, as Moonbeam came over to sniff her outstretched hand hopefully.

"And which of your students had already tried?" Feargal added with a smile. "You forget, Tamsin, I have a mole in the police station! I've already got the gist of the post mortem."

"You weasel! Why didn't you tell us?" Tamsin quickly reviewed what she'd said, and wondered if Feargal had got the whole story or just the scandalous part. "Spill the beans, Feargal!"

"It seems our Gabrielle was stuffed to the gills with poison. She was doomed. And that's why she felt so sick and faint. I have a tiny sneaky feeling you've already learnt that from your chum Maggie, am I right?"

Tamsin smiled beatifically and stayed silent.

"Ok. Let's put our cards on the table. Gabrielle had consumed Death Cap Mushroom. Only a very small amount is deadly. So she could have eaten it in error when picking mushrooms herself, or it could have been slipped into her food by the killer."

"So we just have to find out where she ate that day, and we've got 'em!" said Emerald, her face lighting up for the first time in a while.

"Not necessarily. It could have been put into her food - at her home. Or someone could have hidden it in her lunchbox sandwich at the shop. Or ..."

"Or it could have been mixed in with some other mushrooms, that she'd bought or picked .."

"Or which were given to her!"

Emerald looked deflated again, and put a hand to her forehead. "Maggie's right - it's a question of why. Why on earth would anyone want to kill her."

"Murder usually comes from jealousy, or rage, or needing to silence someone."

"Or money. Don't forget money."

"And you're right, Emerald, we need to find a whole lot more out about Gabrielle, in order to get an idea of who stood to gain if she died .."

"Or lose if she stayed alive." Tamsin finished Feargal's sentence for him.

"You're going to interview The Cake Stop crowd, Feargal? I can do some nosing about at the health shop. I know the place slightly from going in there for organic flour and aloe vera for the dogs. I've seen Barry before."

Feargal's pen stayed poised over his notebook as he waited for elucidation.

"Barry's the manager," said Tamsin. "Emerald thinks Gabrielle had a brother over Gloucester direction - can you find out for us, Feargal? Then we can go and visit him, offer our condolences and the like."

"Ok," and he jotted down another note.

"As for all the students," Tamsin turned to Emerald and held up her hand, "yes, we do have to talk to them. I think Emerald and I can talk to each of them individually. Do you know, some of them are my dog training students too, so I already know several of them."

"I can't believe any of them could have done this," wailed Emerald, still unwilling to lift her protective arm from her loyal students.

"Maybe they didn't! But we need to find out just what they know. What they saw or felt on the night, and anything they'd picked up before then."

"You never know when we might get a crucial bit of info," said Feargal encouragingly.

"And we never know when you're going to come out with one of your shafts of insight!" added Tamsin.

Emerald cheered visibly, snuggling her nose into Opal's creamy fur again.

"We'll sort this, don't you worry," said Feargal. "Maybe your business will get the same fillip Tamsin's did once she emerged without stain!" and he helped himself to the last biscuit.

Chapter 7

"I've got a lunchtime class in Malvern, how about you?" Tamsin was being more solicitous than usual with her house-mate, who was taking the whole thing pretty badly.

"Not much. Two more people have cancelled their sessions for outlandish reasons. I'm hoping they'll come back once this has all died down."

"Maybe if they're that fickle, they're not really the right people for you?" ventured Tamsin.

"You're right, of course. But I do need the money!"

"It's a blip. It'll be fine. So are you working today?"

"Yes, fortunately I have two still happening today .. I need to get going to the first."

"Great! So why don't we meet here after your second session and we can start visiting people? I thought Saffron would be a good bet to start with - she's probably always at home with her baby. Where does she live?"

"Um," Emerald flicked through her bookings folder. "Upton. Out that way. It'll be the other side of Upton, in fact."

"Not across that narrow old Severn bridge that's always having roadworks?"

"Or getting caravans stuck on it! No, the other way. The Pershore road. One of those little villages off the main road."

"Ok, we can start there, and pick up Shirley on the way back. Remember we went there before?"

"I do - the Spanish Hacienda house!"

So they met a few hours later - Emerald in much better spirits after spending so much time doing yoga, and Tamsin having done her puppy class and walked the dogs - and they set off in the trusty van together towards Upton.

They eventually found Saffron's house along the back roads, after pausing at every cottage to read the sometimes barely legible signs - Rose Cottage, End Cottage, Bramley Cottage, so many cottages.

"Really, if they're going to call their house Blossom Cottage, they could at least indicate which end of the village it is," said Tamsin with exasperation, as they at last pulled in and got out of the van. "Who'd be a postman?"

"It's very quiet," said Emerald. "We'd better not wake the baby!"

"Let's knock quietly," and Tamsin made a discreet tap-tap on the window by the front door. An explosion of yapping reassured them that if the baby woke up, it wasn't down to them.

"Napoleon!" they could hear, "Quiet!", then the door opened to reveal Saffron in tracky bottoms and a loose jumper, her hair unkempt and dark rings under her eyes. She peered at Tamsin with vague recollection, then saw Emerald and her face opened up. "Oh hi Emerald - come in. Sorry for the mess," she added automatically as she shepherded little Napoleon ahead of her back to the kitchen. "I was just having a nap. They say you should always sleep when the baby sleeps, and he didn't do much of that last night, so .." she pulled out a couple of chairs at the kitchen table, snatching away the remains of her lunch and her nappy basket complete with dirty nappy, "I've been playing catch-up." She blushed and grabbed a cloth to wipe down the table before saying, "Like a cuppa?

I have to drink masses to keep my milk flowing," she beamed.

Tamsin gritted her teeth against the threatened onslaught of intimate physical details about childbirth and babies, smiled sweetly and said, "Yes please!" She could talk about bitches, mating, puppies and whelping all day long, but she drew the line at human babies!

"Here, you sit down and rest. Let me," said Emerald, jumping up and filling the kettle. "Cups?"

Saffron waved her hand towards the cupboard above the kettle and sank gratefully into a chair, leaning her elbows heavily on the table. "I had no idea having a baby would be so exhausting," she said apologetically.

"Does your husband help?"

"What husband?" she smiled wanly. "Did a runner as soon as he learnt I was pregnant. We weren't married, more fool me."

"I'm sorry to hear that. So you're on your own with ...?"

"Charlie!" Saffron's face brightened instantly. "Yes, just me and him. And Napoleon here. And Fuzzy Bear!" she laughed. "Mustn't forget Fuzzy Bear! All would be lost without Fuzzy Bear." She smiled at

Emerald as she brought cups and saucers to the table. "So to stop myself getting fatter and fatter and becoming a baby-bore, I thought I should get myself in shape. That's why I started back to yoga!"

After a bit of rummaging in the fridge for the milk, Emerald arrived with the teapot and sat to join them. "So where's Charlie now? How does he sleep through Napoleon's barking?"

"He went down a while ago, and after last night's shenanigans he went out like a light. Thank goodness. He's such a lovely little fella - he's usually such a good baby. I hope he isn't sickening for something ..."

"It must be hard on your own, Saffron?" said Tamsin quietly.

Saffron straightened up in her chair. "I'll be back to work in a couple of months, so I want to make the most of this time with Charlie while I can. I love it really. Just tired after last night."

"How will you manage Charlie when you're working?"

"I'm a design consultant, so fortunately I can do a lot from home. But I'll need to arrange daycare one way or another. Need to stay professional," she laughed. "But I expect you haven't come to hear all about me? Is it about that poor girl? I heard it on the local news."

"Yes, we're trying to find out all we can about Gabrielle. It's important that her friends and family know what happened - and it's hard to find anything out about them."

"I can't help you there. I barely knew her," Saffron said quietly as she folded her arms and leant back in her chair.

Seeing this classic evasion technique, Tamsin persisted. "I see you have some jars of nuts over there - do you get them from the health shop in Malvern?"

A look of understanding crossed Saffron's face. "Ohhh, that's where I'd seen her before. Got it. Sorry - Mummy-brain," she giggled, rather unattractively, Tamsin thought.

"Yes! She worked there in the health shop. Very keen on natural foods, home remedies, that kind of thing, you know?" chipped in Emerald.

"I remember now. Yes - I do go there from time to time. Trying to eat the right things for Charlie. You know if you eat the wrong food, it can go through the milk and affect the baby .."

Tamsin clattered her cup on her saucer in an attempt to steer the conversation away from the quality and quantity of Saffron's milk supply, "Oops, sorry!"

Saffron glanced at her. "She was very helpful. Yes. She knew all about which things could provoke allergies in a baby, things to help us both sleep. She looked so different with her hair scraped back into that funny hair-net thing they wear, and in that green overall. Seemed to have something going with that guy."

"Barry?"

"Is that his name? The manager, I think he is. Let's say they seemed to have an understanding ..."

"You think they were an item?" asked Emerald.

"Oh I don't know about that. Maybe she was the sort of woman who has flocks of men around her, I don't know. She was good-looking alright. Looked very different in her yoga gear and with her hair loose. Quite the vamp!"

Tamsin and Emerald kept silent, in case more bitchiness was on the way.

But Saffron, perhaps sensing what they were thinking, changed tack: "I wonder what she'd taken then, that made her so ill? Maybe one of her 'natural remedies'! She looked awful, quite green and pasty. They said that she fell off the fire escape. Whatever was she doing out there?"

"We wondered if you knew - if you might have seen something, heard something ..."

Saffron frowned, apparently thinking hard. Whether she was thinking what to say, or what not to say, they would never know, as at that moment some strange distorted tinny sounds emerged from a speaker on the kitchen worktop, and Saffron jumped to her feet, two round dark stains forming on the front of her t-shirt, saying, "There he is now! My Charlie. He's waking up! You'll want to meet him, won't you!"

"Of course," said Tamsin, gulping down the rest of her tea. "There's just time to say hello before we whiz off!"

They heard Saffron coo-ing and laughing, weirdly distorted through the babyminder gadget, as she fetched her baby from his room, bearing him proudly back into the kitchen, beaming from ear to ear with pride. The baby stared at them blank-faced with his big brown eyes, then turned and started to nuzzle his mother's front.

"What a gorgeous baby!" said Emerald dutifully, leaning forward to touch the baby's clammy olive brown cheek, his wispy black hair stuck to his hot head.

"Lovely! Hello Charlie. We'll leave you to it," Tamsin steered Emerald to the door. "Lovely to meet you both properly. If you think of anything - anything at all which will help us find her friends, you can give us a ring. You know Emerald's number, of course, and here's mine." She placed one of her business cards on the table.

"Oh, you're a dog trainer! We must get you to stop Napoleon barking, mustn't we Charlie-warlie?" and the two visitors slid out of the house.

They set off for Shirley's house. "I didn't know you were so averse to bodily functions?" teased Emerald in the van. "You're always going on about the right diet for your dogs, and what state their poos are."

"That's dogs." said Tamsin firmly, "and puppies. Totally gorgeous. I can talk about them all day! Other people's babies and milk production - that's quite another thing." But she did allow herself a smile.

"Not planning any babies for yourself?"

"No way! I'm very happy being single and child-free. Unencumbered with other people. Sebastian pushing off when he did was a blessing in disguise. So much better now."

Emerald gazed out of the window as the hedgerows whooshed by. "I think we could have been stuck there for hours, as an audience of the holy feeding. Just as well you bolted when you did!"

"Shirley will be a very different kettle of fish. Remember her?"

"Wasn't she the one with the huge white dog?"

"That's the one! Remember she was always pretty offhand?"

"For good reason, as it turned out!" nodded Emerald as she remembered the happenings in Nether Trotley earlier that year, and as they passed between the menacingly tall hedges either side of Shirley's front gate and pulled into the long drive, the huge white dog roused himself from the front terrace and started a deep regular woof.

By the time they were ready to get out of the car, Shirley had arrived and taken Luke by the collar. "Hi Shirley, Hello Luke!" And the big dog's tail started to wave as his owner let go of his collar and, mouth relaxed and tongue lolling, he went to greet the visitor who he recognised well from his classes.

As ever, Shirley looked nervous and withdrawn. She'd spent so much of her life hiding, hiding her family, that she didn't relax easily. "Hello Tamsin, Hello Emerald. And what brings you two ladies here, or can I guess?"

"It looks as though we seem to have a knack of being in the wrong place at the wrong time," laughed Tamsin.

"Or of running classes full of homicidal maniacs?" Shirley raised an eyebrow in the nearest thing to a tease Tamsin had ever seen in her, as she indicated the long verandah at the front of the house, and the table they had sat at last time they visited.

"It's beginning to look that way!" laughed Tamsin and drew her coat under her as they all sat on the cold metal chairs. "But why do you think there's a homicidal maniac at large in the yoga fraternity?"

"Oh! Well, if she'd just fallen off that fire escape because she felt dizzy - and she looked pretty ropy in class I can tell you: I kept thinking she was about to throw up on my mat! - then I think somehow you wouldn't be here." Shirley gazed shrewdly at Tamsin.

"There's no flies on you, Shirley Vaughan!" Tamsin laughed to lighten the conversation. "Honestly, we've no idea what happened to the poor girl. But Emerald feels she has some responsibility to get in touch with people Gabrielle knew .."

Emerald smiled obligingly. "I do."

"I can't see it's your fault, Emerald, any more than that other business was Tamsin's fault. Weird, that .." Shirley's mind was clearly revisiting the Nether Trotley affair.

"I keep telling her that! But we wondered if you happened to know anything about Gabrielle - outside class, you know?"

"I've only been to that shop she worked in a few times. I like to get my organic flour there for baking,"

"You bake?" asked Tamsin in honest surprise.

"I do indeed. It's quite a thing of mine actually. Mark does love my baking," Shirley smiled coyly. "Anyway, I go there for flour. And I'll say this much - you see some strange people in there sometimes. And there's a large stock of dried herbs ... *of every sort.*" She shut her mouth and gave them knowing looks.

"You think the shop's promoting legal highs?"

"Ooh I didn't say that," Shirley backtracked fast.

And they all relapsed into silence as they mulled over these thoughts.

"I believe," began Shirley thoughtfully, "she had a brother. She mentioned it once. She misunderstood when I said where I lived and she thought I'd said Redmarley, and did I know her brother? So that may be a clue for you Tamsin," she grinned as she stood up. Luke lumbered to his feet and Tamsin held her hand out towards his big head. He sniffed it and walked away.

"Can't win 'em all," she smiled. "He's growing into a lovely dog."

"A discerning dog," laughed Emerald, as they headed to the van, waving a cheery goodbye to Shirley.

"I've never heard her talk so much!" said Tamsin as she negotiated the exit in the tall hedge onto the quiet road. "I guess she was so anxious about the Trotley thing that she stayed buttoned up the whole time."

"What do you think of what she said about the herbs?"

"Hmm, if you add in Saffron's suggestion of Gabrielle and Barry being thick as thieves, it certainly gives us something to look into. I wonder if smoking herbs is a gateway to hard drug use."

"Feargal will know that, I'm sure."

"It may be that someone didn't want this info getting out? Let's have a go at Barry right now!" and Tamsin pointed her trusty van back towards Great Malvern.

Chapter 8

The town was busy and noisy, the monthly market full of local produce cluttering up the street under the Priory archway - the splendid entrance and only remaining building of the Benedictine Priory founded in 1086, built at a time when Henry VII and later Henry VIII visited their hunting grounds in Malvern. The green and white striped awnings over the stalls made a pretty sight, and people bustled from one stand to another, sampling the goodies and purchasing their weekly shop. Tamsin was greeted enthusiastically by a man with a dog hauling him along the path. "See you next week at class!" she laughed, shaking her head gently.

They reached the health shop, right next to the busy market, which was also boasting baskets of fresh food along the pavement in front of its large front window.

Inside, Barry was looking hot and bothered as he repeated some instructions, very slowly, to a gormless-looking girl who was more concerned with getting her hairnet in a more flattering position than in listening to her new boss.

He looked up with some relief as the bell jangled and Tamsin and Emerald came into the shop. His frustrated expression turned to smarmy effusiveness as he muttered to the girl, "Just clean the worktops, Rose," and then turned to welcome his customers with a big smile pasted onto his face.

"Hello, Barry, isn't it?" Tamsin began.

"I'm Barry, yes," he smiled broadly. "What can I do for you ladies today? We have a new delivery of organic apples just arrived .."

"Actually, we're here about Gabrielle."

"Oh. Gabrielle. Such a loss," he switched on his caring expression as he glanced over to Rose who was presumably Gabrielle's ill-chosen replacement. "Very sad. Very sad."

"Had she been here long?" asked Emerald with sympathy.

"About three years. Yes. Three years. She was very good. Very interested in natural living." He shook his head slowly. "Great loss." He jumped at a crash from the kitchen area as Rose hastily scooped up the metal bowl she'd knocked on the floor and carried on idly wiping the worktop with a nonchalant look on her face. He raised his eyebrows and stared at the floor for a moment.

"You see, I was her yoga teacher, and we were wanting to get in touch with any of her friends or relatives. Tell them the inside story."

"There's an inside story?" Barry asked sharply.

"Oh no, I mean, just to talk to them about Gabrielle and what happened .."

"Not that we know much about what *did* happen," Tamsin put in quickly, not wanting to impart any information to Barry. "I gather she has a brother?"

"Oh yes, she has ... er, had. I've got his number here somewhere." He pulled his phone out of the pocket of his green coat. "She'd stay the weekend with him sometimes ... ermm ... she gave me his number just in case, you know? Er, here it is. Alphonse. Strange name ..." He turned the phone to face them and Tamsin quickly scribbled down the number.

"Thanks. We'll get in touch with him. You say Gabrielle was into natural living - was she well up in the things you sell? She seemed to know all about dried beans when I came in here once!"

"Oh yes, she made a study of these things - specially keen on natural remedies. Hated doctors!"

That explains why she didn't seek help quickly, Tamsin thought to herself, as Emerald - who had drifted over to the well-stocked leaflets rack - came back holding up a flyer announcing a 'Food for Free' workshop.

"Was she into this kind of thing? Foraging, roadkill, and all that?" she asked.

"She was, yes, indeed she was. I told her it wasn't good for business, teaching people how they could eat for free!" He guffawed at his joke while his audience remained straightfaced. "But she insisted on putting out the flyers. I can get rid of them now," he smiled. "Some friend of hers was running that workshop. He goes about The Three Counties giving them."

Tamsin smiled at the mention of the local name for Herefordshire, Gloucestershire and Worcestershire. "That's interesting. I've always wanted to know more about that. Let me see - oh, it's on Saturday! I may go," and she took the flyer from Emerald's outstretched hand and pocketed it before Barry could ditch it along with the rest of them.

"So did Gabrielle eat a lot of her own foraged food?" asked Emerald sweetly. "I mean you'd need to be a bit of an expert, wouldn't you, so you didn't pick the wrong thing?"

"That's a point! It's surprising that she fell to her death because she was feeling sick and dizzy ..." added Tamsin. "Do you think she ate something she shouldn't have?"

"I heard that alright," Barry shifted from one foot to the other, looking very uncomfortable.

"Who from?" interjected Tamsin.

"Oh, one of our customers," said Barry airily, waving his hand around as if to indicate a swelling throng of people in the shop. Hard to imagine. She really did know her stuff. She wanted to bring some berries and fungi here to sell but I said 'no way'! I wasn't going to risk someone keeling over on me!" He laughed loudly, his fat shoulders bouncing up and down.

Emerald was wandering again, and stood in front of a display of dried herbs. "I've never seen so many herbs! Do you specialise in them?"

"Er yes, we do, as a matter of fact. We're well known in the area for our range. They're all organic, you know ..." he started eagerly into his sales spiel, and as Tamsin went over to look at the herb display, the shop phone rang. Rose answered it and they heard her say, "Gabrielle? No. She ain't here any more ... I dunno, do I? ... D'you want to talk to Barry? Hello? Hello?" She peered at the phone, shrugged her shoulders and slammed it back on its rest, giving it a quick clean while she was at it and smiling sweetly at her manager.

"Who was that?" asked Barry.

"Dunno. They rung off, didn't they."

"I need to teach you how we answer the phone, Rose," he sighed and turned back to Tamsin and Emerald, in time to hear the bell jangle and see the front door closing behind them.

"This gets weirder," said Tamsin once they were out on the street and their feet were taking them up towards The Cake Stop, as if on auto-pilot.

"At least we have the brother's phone number."

"Alphonse. Wonder where the family originates?"

"I always thought she had a South American look about her."

"Wouldn't that make him 'Alfonso'?"

"And she'd be 'Gabriela'. Perhaps they thought a French name sounded better? Perhaps they had a French mother? Who knows!" said Emerald, pushing open the café door.

They settled at a corner table with the coffees Kylie made for them, and a large slice of yet another creation of the Furies' - Pistachio and Caramel - to share. "We deserve this, after our investigating!" said Tamsin as she shovelled a loaded spoonful of bliss into her mouth.

"*Mais bonjour, mes amies!*" Jean-Philippe strode over to their table and sat down in the third armchair. "Any more deaths for me? I've had it up to here with police tape and questioning," he held his hand up to his neck, moving it in a sawing motion.

"I'm so sorry, Jean-Philippe," Emerald began, looking both sad and guilty. "I absolutely understand if you want me to take my class elsewhere ..."

"*Pas du tout!* You did not kill her, *ma petite!* I know you didn't want this to happen. It's just one of those things. The unfortunate lady happened to be here when she was overcome."

Tamsin and Emerald exchanged glances. "There's a little more to it than that,"

Jean-Philippe groaned. "Oh no, not another of your murders?"

"Actually, yes. It does look that way." Tamsin quickly recalled what she'd promised Maggie not to divulge and started in on the rest. She spoke quietly, so that the café's mood-music would prevent her being overheard. "It seems she was suffering from fatal mushroom poisoning. If she hadn't landed in your yard she'd have been dead in a few more days. She hated doctors, so it would have been too late to save her by the time she collapsed from liver failure."

"*Mon Dieu!* But that's *terrible!* And she such a lovely young girl. How did she come to eat poisonous mushrooms? They must be hard to find?"

"No, you can find them all over the place apparently. But the strange thing is that she was a bit of an expert in foraging for food. It's hard to believe she'd have knowingly eaten a Death Cap herself."

"Death Cap!" said Jean-Philippe, and shuddered. "Ah! *Je comprends! Le Calice du Mort* - the Chalice of Death."

Emerald closed her eyes for a moment. "And you only need a very small bit for it to be terminal."

"So … what you're saying is, that someone secretly administered this poison to her?"

"It looks that way."

"And," Emerald looked about her before whispering, "we're not sure she *fell*."

Jean-Philippe's large bushy black eyebrows went a further inch up his forehead. "No wonder the police are here all the time. They've spent ages on the fire escape and the yard, all wearing their paper suits. They've taken the tape away now, so Kylie can get her bike out at last."

"We've been talking to people."

"People from my class."

"And from the shop she worked in - you know, the health shop?"

"*Bien,* that worked very well for you last time round - talking to people."

"Last two times!" Emerald laughed. "Don't forget Tamsin's the Malvern Hills Detective!"

"*Alors,* the Malvern Hills Detective has no sniffer dog with her today."

Tamsin grinned. "I walked them earlier. No point in shoving them in the van for the afternoon while we ... "

".. eat cake!" Jean-Philippe nodded to the now clean plates. "How do you like this one, by the way? Damaris says it's a new recipe."

"Gorgeous," said Emerald.

"Just what a hungry detective needs after a hard day of sleuthing!" laughed Tamsin.

"So who are you going to talk to next?"

"We're going after the brother. They were quite close, it seems. He must know something. If she didn't willingly eat those mushrooms, then someone fed them to her."

"You say she didn't fall - you know this?"

"No." Tamsin lied firmly, crossing her fingers at the same time. "It just seems unlikely that someone feeling so weak could have jettisoned themselves over that high balustrade."

Jean-Philippe looked very serious as he said, "Then we need to find out what happened. A lovely young woman ... *c'est monstrueux.*"

"Monstrous indeed."

"Can you keep your eyes peeled, Jean-Philippe?" said Emerald. "You're in a great position to pick up info."

"I will. And listen - this is someone with an evil mind you are looking to catch. Promise me you'll take care."

"Promise," they chorused solemnly. And they were not to know how quickly they were going to break that promise.

Chapter 9

Tamsin drove up to Bishop's Green's pretty village green and was happy to be there again - this time without any fears of homicidal maniacs, all such maniacs now being lodged safely at His Majesty's Pleasure.

The splendid trees surrounding the green were tinged with red and yellow now, and a carpet of rich-coloured leaves lay beneath each tree, coating the ground too round the small green-painted wooden cricket pavilion. It was almost tempting enough to get her to go and kick through the leaves, letting out her inner child!

But instead she turned her attention to No.1, The Cottages, where she had come to catch up with Julia and her hitherto troublesome Miniature

Schnauzer Romeo. Julia had been in touch a week before, as it happened, requesting another training session, and it was a Heaven-sent opportunity for Tamsin to do some more snooping. This time about the yoga class.

Tamsin was seriously impressed when the door was opened to reveal a proud Julia with Romeo sitting beside her - trembling with excitement, but silent, and she told Julia so.

"Fantastic! You've worked so hard with him."

"It's made all the difference, Tamsin! We feel as if we're on the same side now," and they went through to the kitchen to work on the tricks Julia had begun teaching her little dog with a few choice tips, quickly ironing out where she had got stuck.

After the session, by which time Romeo was readily fetching his lead from its shelf and holding it still for Julia to take then clip to his collar, Julia said, "Oh you clever little munchkin, Romeo! Time for coffee," and put the kettle on so they could switch to chat.

"Well!" she began, "You seem to be a magnet for violent deaths, Tamsin!"

"Don't remind me," sighed Tamsin. "But to be fair, this is Emerald's class, not mine."

"But you were there beforehand - you met us all there."

"Yeah, and I was surprised to see you! I didn't realise you did yoga with Emerald."

"Not just me, but when Sara's around I give her a lift over too."

"How's she doing at College?"

"Loving it! So far as I can see she spends most of the day messing about with her mare Crystal. Heaven for her."

"I'd love to see her again, when's she next home?"

"She's back now. Half-term hols. My two are off as well, but they've gone to tennis. I'll have to collect them later."

"Not archery?"

"Ah, archery's slightly less popular round here than it used to be," she smiled, bringing dimples to her cheeks. "Though the galloping major still runs his classes. Tell you what, I'll give Sara a buzz, I'm sure she's got loads to tell you." And she grabbed her phone and dashed off a text.

So it wasn't long before the front door opened and in came Sara, ruffling Romeo's hairy ears down the hallway.

"That was quick! No horse - how did you do it?"

"I snitched one of the men's bikes. Gotta get it back before they clock off!" and after some enthusiastic catching-up with Tamsin, she said, "Tell me what happened. Gabrielle was a lovely girl. It's too awful. That's the second person I know who's met a horrible end."

"It *is* awful, you're right. How much do you know?"

"Just that she felt ill and fell off the fire escape ... there's more?"

"'Fraid so. You know she was into all things natural? Well it seems that the reason she felt so ill was that she'd eaten poisonous mushrooms."

Tamsin's friends sat, mouths open, staring at her.

"The awful thing is that she would have died anyway, in a few days. This was just the beginning."

"So she ate some toadstools? And that's why she fell?"

"Er, no. She'd ingested the poison alright. But it seems she couldn't have actually fallen in a faint over that balustrade. Not on her own." She was determined not to give away Maggie's secret information about the buckle mark.

Their mouths gaped further.

"Someone pushed her over?"

"It's hard to imagine how else it could have happened."

"Oh no, poor Gabrielle," Sara pressed her palms to her cheeks.

"Now Emerald's terribly upset. She's afraid everyone will leave her classes in droves."

"Of course," they chorused with concern. "But we won't leave, will we, Julia?" They both shook their heads vigorously.

"I wouldn't miss it for anything!" said Julia. "Tell Emerald we'll be there on Tuesday."

"She'll be so pleased! And so, you see, I want to find out what I can, to show that it wasn't her fault."

"And you can't resist it!" laughed Sara.

"True - you know me too well!" Tamsin grinned. "So I wondered - you knew Gabrielle. What was she like?"

Julia began. "She was lovely - really good at yoga. She was into salads and raw foods and whatnot. Must help if you don't eat chocolate and cake all day," she smirked, patting her own slender form. "And she has a brother - had a brother - who's something to do with horses. Do you know what, Sara?"

"I think he does a bit of livery, and rides some hurdles. She went down for weekends sometimes, I believe. And she was quite a serious person," added Sara. "Into saving whales and stuff, if you know what I mean."

"She'd have got on with your environmentalist friends?"

"She probably did, for all I know. It's quite a network. Yes, anything natural she was into."

"Do you know about the foraging workshops she was promoting? Some friend of hers?"

"Ye-e-es, she did mention them. She was keen on finding free food - 'Nature's Bounty' she'd always call it." Sara sighed.

"Yes, she loved Autumn, because there are so many fruits and berries .."

"And it's the mushroom season," said Tamsin. They all fell silent for a moment.

"But she was serious, as I said," Sara piped up. "She would surely not have picked a poisonous mushroom! She was always using that app on her phone to identify growing things. She showed me one day. She thought I may find it useful for Crystal."

"And from what I've heard, no, she wouldn't have knowingly eaten a Death Cap." Tamsin saw both her friends shiver.

"You mean someone poisoned her? And then someone else pushed her to her death?"

"Two people wanted her dead? It beggars belief," snorted Julia.

After a pause, Tamsin asked, "Who do you think might want her .. out of the way? And why?"

"I went to her health shop a couple of times," Sara said, "and saw some fairly shifty-looking people stocking up on the herbs. I wonder if there was something going on there, and she knew too much?"

"Do you know anything about herbs used as legal highs?"

"Yeah. There are idiots at College who smoke them. It's a slippery slope, you know."

"A 'gateway drug'?" asked Julia with a frown. "I've been boning up on them now Francine is going off to Hereford on the school bus every day. I didn't realise they could use herbs ..."

"Cannabis and tobacco are plants too," said Sara, with her land conservation studies in mind. "Hey!" she sat upright suddenly, "some horses have tested positive for herbs. You know, when they do the doping tests? There are some herbs that people have used - and come unstuck."

Julia put down her mug with a bang, eliciting a "wuff" from Romeo who had been asleep on his bed. "The brother! Think something was going on there?"

"Herbs and drugs ... that would certainly point to big money. Someone could well have taken the risk if they thought their plan had been found out!" Tamsin leant forward in her chair.

"But the mushroom must have been picked by someone with knowledge. I mean, I wouldn't have a clue which mushroom to pick!" Julia shrugged.

"That would narrow the field a good bit ..." agreed Sara.

"What about her friends at the class?"

"You don't think it was one of us?" Julia was horrified.

"Not one of you two, silly! But who else was there?"

"That Kurt is a bit weird. Was he there that night?" Sara asked Julia.

"He was, yes. And he always stays apart - doesn't mix with us at all. But he looks so much like a caricature of a criminal, maybe he's the exact opposite!"

"Jane and Alice are scatterbrained. I can't imagine them having anything to do with anything nefarious."

"What about your chum Andrew?"

"He's not my chum! I mean, he's nice enough, and I know he fancies me, but that's as far as it goes. He bounds about like a big puppy and looks as though he's about to say 'Who's for tennis?' I've never seen him paying much attention to Gabrielle though?"

"That Shirley is a bit of a dark horse, don't you think? Always a bit self-contained. I wonder .."

Tamsin decided to keep silent about her dog training student.

"Who else? Oh, there's Harry."

"*Harry!*" Sara laughed.

"What's so funny about Harry?"

"He's always so scatterbrained - I can't imagine him as a master-criminal! He's always tripping over his own feet."

"He did like Gabrielle though. I saw him looking at her sometimes, in the café," Julia put in. "He'd look suddenly very together and serious. A bit dark, almost." She shuddered.

Tamsin was making mental notes of all this. "And what about Linda? And Saffron?"

"Linda's been coming to class for ages. It's amazing how supple and bendy she is - specially at her age. But I can't see her hurling young women over balustrades." Julia put her chin in her hands, elbows on table.

"And Saffron - all she talks about is babies!" Sara said, as dismissively as only a teenager could.

Julia said, "But we all went out together. At the end of class."

"Except Gabrielle."

"Except Gabrielle, of course. But I mean, the rest of us - we were all there. I'm pretty sure of it."

"Can you have a think, Julia? Can you remember what order you left? Who went down the stairs first, or last?"

"I'll turn it over in my mind. It's not exactly memorable. But I find things can suddenly pop back into your head if you leave them alone."

"You'll tell me what you remember?"

"Course! There was I thinking it was a simple accident, and now it seems it's a brutal murder."

"That's what Tamsin deals in!" laughed Sara. "Hey, I'd better be getting that bike back home. I'll be able to come to class this week - wouldn't miss it! Ok for a lift, Julia?"

And they all made their goodbyes.

Chapter 10

It wasn't yet lunchtime, so Tamsin decided to scoot home and walk the dogs, then take Emerald over to Lower Thatchall to see Molly, and on towards Gloucester to see if they could catch Harry at home.

The weather was very October-ish, cold and sharp with a hint of frost which left the grass soaking wet and sparkling as the sun tried to break through. The Malvern Hills looked distant and misty as they towered over the town, and Tamsin had worked up quite an appetite by the time she turned homewards.

"Hey, that's lovely!" she said as she arrived back from her cold damp walk with three hot, but also damp, dogs. As she towelled many paws, she saw Emerald putting the finishing touches to two salady wraps, and pushing down the plunger on the cafetiere.

"Thought this would speed things up a bit. And anyway, I'm so glad you're helping with this. It's all so awful."

"Any more wobblers?"

"Yes. One of my clients who hates travel and never goes anywhere is suddenly going 'out of town'. It's depressing. And worrying."

"I know just how you feel! Don't worry, we'll sort this, and you'll surge ahead again. I got a lot of bookings out of pure curiosity after the Bishop's Green debacle. Once Feargal's piece came out."

"Have you heard from him yet, about the brother?"

"Not yet. But we will." And Tamsin tucked into her lunch with gusto as she warmed up from the coffee.

"So Molly is another of your students?" asked Emerald as they finished their meal.

"Yes, no - well actually it was her husband Chas who would come to the classes with the three boys. Their baby was still quite young. Nice family! And they're pretty sharp, so if there was anything to notice, they'll have noticed it."

"Cameron is how old? Nine?"

"Something like that."

"He's very bendy, of course. Supple. But he actually works hard at class. I took him on for one class to see, in case he was disruptive. But he's not at all."

"He's very bright, I seem to remember."

"I wonder what he will have noticed …"

And Emerald didn't have to wonder for long. The sun had faded and the damp day was misty again, so Tamsin had her headlights on. There weren't all that many cars about this dull afternoon. They rolled through the old-fashioned Main Street of Lower Thatchall and pulled up at Molly's large modern house. As before, they had to negotiate abandoned bikes and scooters in the front garden, but as soon as they arrived at the front door of the house, Cameron raced up to them and shouted, "I know who killed Gabrielle!"

"Yeah, we know!" echoed Alex, who as ever could not stand still, and was hopping and pirouetting on the spot, as was Buster the Jack Russell, who was delighted to greet Tamsin again.

Little Joe pushed himself in front of his brothers, puffed out his chest proudly and said, "I know too!"

"Goodness, why do you think anyone killed her? Wasn't it an accident?" asked Tamsin, looking across at Molly with a raised eyebrow.

"Yes, it was an accident, boys. A very sad accident," Molly said calmly to her brood while she shepherded them all back into the kitchen, adding "Chas has run down to the shops with Amanda. He won't be long."

"But Tamsin's here, so it must be murder!" retorted Cameron with impeccable logic.

Tamsin smiled and crossed her fingers behind her back. "Sorry to disappoint you boys, but it seems the poor girl just fell." She had no intention of giving these children nightmares.

"But I *saw* him!" persisted Cameron.

"Who did you see, darling?" asked Molly with consternation.

"That man, that big man ... um, Kurt! I saw him when we left."

"Come and sit down here, Cameron, and tell us just what you saw, and when."

Cameron sat at the table, while his two lieutenants shuffled along on the bench either side of him.

"Ok. When we left, I ran down the stairs first. I like to jump down the last step and skid on the shiny floor." He glanced across under his lashes to his mother, remembering how often she'd told him not to. "And Kurt was just going out through the door. He walks really fast. So I ran up and waited in the doorway for Mum, and I *saw* him!"

"Saw him what?" asked Tamsin keenly.

"I saw him walk to the end of The Cake Stop then go down the alley." He sat back, triumphant.

"And then what did he do?"

"I dunno." Cameron looked forlorn. "But I know that you can get to the back of The Cake Stop that way. I went and had a look one day while Mum was gossiping with someone." Molly raised her eyebrows but said nothing. "And that must be where the fire escape goes. There's no point in a fire escape if you can't escape on it," he added, with yet more impeccable logic.

"That's true, Cameron. You can get to the back via that alley. I expect that's how those big bins get emptied. But do you know where else the alley goes?"

"No." Cameron looked glum.

Emerald piped up, "I think the alley goes all along the back of that run of buildings. There are flats above most of the shops. Maybe Kurt was visiting someone?"

"Do you know his address?" asked Molly.

"Let me have a look." Emerald hunted in her phone, and found his address. It's 37 Plowman Street. Isn't that near that gym? Hey, doesn't Plowman Street run behind the road The Cake Stop's in?"

"It does. So presumably that's a shortcut home to his own flat. The back gardens of Plowman Street must access the alley. Let's have a look at the map. Can you get it up on your phone, Emerald?"

To lessen Cameron's evident disappointment, Tamsin said, "I think that's really observant of you Cameron - you'll make a fine detective. But it looks as though Kurt may have an alibi for being in the alley."

"He could still have gone to the fire escape," said Alex, not wishing to let this go so easily.

"You're quite right, he could. But tell me - why do you think anyone wanted to hurt Gabrielle?"

"Mum was watching this awful film the other day, you know - kissing and stuff," Cameron pulled a face, "and a man got really angry and hit this woman ..."

"That was way past your bedtime! How did you see that?" demanded Molly.

The two older boys looked sideways at each other, then shrugged.

"I'm going to have to rig up an alarm on those stairs!" said Molly.

"So you think Kurt was upset with Gabrielle? Why? Were they special friends?"

"Not really. I don't know. I know who she *is* friends with though," Cameron folded his arms proudly across his little chest.

"*Was*," interrupted Joe. "*Was* friends with. She's not friends with anyone now."

Tamsin chose to ignore this. "Who?"

"That Harry guy. The one who's always dropping things and saying sorry. I think he only comes to yoga to see Gabrielle. He's *useless* at it."

Tamsin glanced at Emerald, who gave a faint nod. "He does struggle with balance."

"And what makes you think Harry had a thing for Gabrielle?"

"He was always watching her. And last week he was the last to come downstairs."

"I was the last, as I shut the door," said Emerald with a puzzled expression.

"Yes, but he went back up. Don't you remember? He said he'd forgotten something and pushed back up the stairs past me. I nearly missed my jump."

Emerald looked stricken. "You're right! I'd quite forgotten. Cameron, you're a marvel." Cameron wriggled on the bench, gave a mock salute, and looked suitably smug.

"How long was he gone, collecting his stuff?" asked Tamsin, trying to keep the urgency out of her voice.

"Oh, not long," said Cameron airily. "He pushed past me again in the doorway when I was waiting for Mum. She was chattering on to Saffron." He smiled charmingly at his mother.

Buster's barking interrupted them and Chas arrived back with his little daughter in one arm and a big bag of shopping in the other, his car keys in his mouth, pushing the door shut with his foot.

The boys were instantly distracted by the possibility of sweets for them in the shopping bag, and Tamsin and Emerald took the opportunity to leave the family to their Saturday and get on their way, Molly, now carrying Amanda on her hip, came to the door with them. "Do you think it really was an accident?" she asked. "I don't think you'd be that interested if it had been."

"We didn't want to alarm the boys," said Tamsin, "but yes, it seems there may have been foul play."

"Then you have a couple of leads to follow up, thanks to young Sherlock here," she smiled. Then she turned to Emerald and said, "We'll be there on Tuesday, don't you worry."

Emerald smiled broadly and held Amanda's chubby hand for a moment, before they departed and walked back towards the van.

"Let's go and see Harry right now. He lives down this way somewhere doesn't he?"

"Yep. On the Gloucester Road. What do you think of all that?"

"*Out of the mouths of babes and little ones*," Tamsin said quietly. "We'll have to talk to Kurt anyway - just to see if he saw anything. Could be very useful."

"Assuming it's not him."

"Always assuming it's not him! Tell me about Harry while I drive." And they both clambered into the Top Dogs van and set off.

Chapter 11

Emerald was filling Tamsin in on her sketchy knowledge of Harry as they drove. "Now I come to think of it, he did join a while after Gabrielle. She'd been coming for a few months when he first showed up. They didn't appear to know each other, but you know what I'm like. I don't see through people."

"On the contrary, you see with shafts of unparalleled brilliance!"

Emerald gave a light laugh. "My brilliance didn't give me any shafts at that stage. But as time went by I did notice that Harry would try to get near to Gabrielle - in the café, you know, but she didn't seem to warm to him. I didn't think anything of it, to be honest."

"Perhaps there was nothing to think?"

"I wonder … Something clearly was going on. I wonder where Harry fits in to all this. Herbs, perhaps? Unrequited love? Something more sinister?"

"We'll soon find out, as I think this must be the place," and Tamsin pulled in to a lay-by in front of a small dilapidated Edwardian house with bay windows either side of the shabby front door and an overgrown front garden. Round the side of the house, past the bedraggled stinging nettles and docks they could see a rather smart shiny car - the speedy sort that young men aspire to.

Harry didn't look best pleased at their unannounced arrival, but accepted their excuse of going to Gloucester and realising they were passing close by. He led them into a dark scruffy living room whose basic old furniture and lack of personal touches made it look like a dentist's waiting room, and whooshed last week's Sunday papers on to the floor to allow them to sit on the sofa.

"We just wanted to know if you can help us," Emerald began, in her sweetest, blondest, way.

"Gabrielle was a lovely girl, and we want to get in touch with her family - perhaps help them get closure," Tamsin rattled the glib expression off her tongue.

"Oh right, I see," Harry said, sitting down in the armchair opposite, stretching his legs out in front of him and kicking the three-legged occasional table that then wobbled precariously before becoming still again.

"So anything you can tell us would be really helpful!"

"Did you know Gabrielle well? Outside of class, I mean?"

"Uh, no, not at all." He cleared his throat. "I didn't know her at all, except for Tuesday nights." He crossed his arms, then crossed his legs too.

Wow! Thought Tamsin, how many blocking body language signals can he give us!

"It's an awful thing …" Emerald tried to open the conversation up again.

"Yes, it is awful. Such a lovely young woman …"

"Yes, and people are now thinking that I kill my students! People are cancelling - it's very upsetting."

"I don't want to upset you further, but I don't think I'll make it this Tuesday. Got, er, got to visit someone that afternoon. Won't be back in time," he ended with an unconvincing grin.

"Oh, what a shame! Still, you've got a few classes in hand, I believe. So I'll look forward to seeing you again next week." Emerald smiled sweetly again, fully aware that Harry would shortly be history as far as yoga was concerned.

"Tell me," said Tamsin, "did you get any idea of why Gabrielle should want to kill herself?"

"Kill herself?" gasped Harry. "But I thought it was an accident!"

"Have you seen how high that balustrade on the fire escape is? It couldn't be an accident. I know the police are asking loads of questions ... have they questioned you?"

"No!" He said sharply. "No, they haven't. I wouldn't have anything to tell them. I had no idea ..."

"Oh, did you find the thing you'd lost?" Emerald changed the subject abruptly.

"Lost?" Harry looked baffled.

"Yes! The thing you went back for last Tuesday, when we'd all left the room."

Harry blushed. "Oh, er, yes - er, my papers. Yes, I got them thanks - totally forgot them! Came straight from a job, you see, so that's why I had them with me. Scatterbrained, that's me!" He gave them a boyish smile.

"So you took your yoga mat and towel to your appointment?" Tamsin smiled back.

"Ah, yes, yes I did." Harry looked uncomfortable.

"So where were they, these papers? I checked the room as always at the end of the session, and I didn't see anything left behind."

Harry's fingers fidgeted on the arms of the chair. "Ah, I'd dropped them behind the door. Wanted to leave them out of the way of the class, you know! You wouldn't have seen them there." He smiled triumphantly, then added, "I say, would you mind awfully? I have to be going out in a few minutes."

"Of course," the women both jumped up from the sofa. "Thanks so much for helping us."

"I helped you?"

"Oh yes," Tamsin smiled, and they left a very puzzled-looking and slightly annoyed young man as they went back to the van.

But once in the van, they could see Harry staring at them from his window, a dark frown on his face. "Better drive towards Gloucester for a bit then cut back a different way," muttered Tamsin as she put the van in gear. "That's one very shifty character. We don't want to give him cause not to believe us."

After their detour, they wove their way through the Wyche Cutting - the narrow gap between the Worcestershire and Herefordshire Beacons - and the huge vista of the Severn valley opened up before them as they descended. Emerald suddenly shouted "Workshop!" Tamsin screeched to an emergency stop, breathed slowly and looked accusingly at her passenger.

"I'm so sorry! I didn't mean to give you a fright," said Emerald apologetically.

As she re-started the engine, Tamsin replied, "Just don't do that again. But you're right - isn't it today?"

"Yes, here," she dug the crumpled Food for Free flyer out of the pocket in the van door. "It's at the Quaker Meeting House. Started a couple of hours ago - we completely forgot!"

"Let's get there now, we'll catch the end of it."

Finding a parking space on the quiet road, they slipped into the back of the old hall for the last bit of the meeting. There were some colourful hippie types, but most of the audience were greyheads in country walking gear. Emerald nudged Tamsin as she spotted the large frame of Kurt halfway down the full rows of seats, listening attentively and taking notes. Tamsin pursed her lips, raised her eyebrows and tilted her head.

The photos of roadkill pinned to the front of the speaker's table rather turned Tamsin's stomach, and she was glad to hear they'd passed that stage of the lecture and were busily discussing mushrooms that members of the audience had found. A kind of "show and tell" session.

It wasn't long before the meeting wound up and most people started chatting animatedly and moving towards the exit. They'd clearly enjoyed their esoteric meeting. Tamsin and Emerald held back and busied themselves with the notices as they could see the tall figure of Kurt heading for the door, walking alone as ever. A few people were asking the speaker more questions and showing him photos on their phone, and Tamsin and Emerald joined the group waiting to talk to the expert.

Colin was clearly tired after giving his Workshop, but turned to them with an interested hello.

"I'm so sorry we didn't arrive till the last minute - we had an engagement before - but what we heard was fascinating!" Tamsin began.

"I'd no idea that there was so much we could eat from the countryside!" smiled Emerald. "We had a friend who was into all this kind of thing - did you know her? Gabrielle."

Colin's face fell. "Oh yes, Gabrielle was a regular attendee at my Workshops. Such a terrible thing. I read about it in the *Malvern Mercury*."

"So she was an avid forager?" asked Tamsin.

"Oh yes, very keen. She was fastidious about studying her subject. Knew all about different species of plants, and how to use them. You know you can make very nutritious soups from the hedgerow? Stinging nettles impart a husky flavour."

"Really? I had no idea! Did Gabrielle know about mushrooms too?" Emerald nodded towards the array of photos of the forest floor.

"Fungi was her *forte*! She actually gave a talk once on how to identify mushrooms - important! You do know some will kill you, don't you?" He peered at them over his glasses with concern.

"Er yes, I just stick to Field Mushrooms. In fields." Tamsin assured him.

"Very wise. You need to know what you're doing if you look for mushrooms in the woods."

"So there's no chance Gabrielle would ever make a mistake over the safety of what she could eat?"

"No chance. She knew her subject. Such a loss. I'll have to find another person, oh dear …"

They thanked the distracted lecturer and went on their way.

"Now we really have learnt something!" Tamsin said triumphantly once she was behind the wheel again. "Gabrielle did not mistake her mushrooms."

"We've learnt two things," Emerald corrected her. "In all probability, neither does Kurt."

Their minds whirred as they thought out the connections, and it wasn't till they'd arrived back in Pippin Lane and were hearing the excited woofing from inside the house that Tamsin said, "But why on earth would Kurt want to poison Gabrielle?"

"When are we visiting him? Monday?"

"Nope. Got class on Monday evening. Tuesday, before your class? We'll have to work something out."

"I wonder what his interest is in Food for Free?" mused Emerald. "He really doesn't look the type, though I know I shouldn't judge people by their appearance."

"I wouldn't have thought he was the yoga type, to be honest. But he is."

"True. True. He can't help how he's built - especially if he's doing heavy manual work all day. He's very good on the strength poses - headstands and arm balances ... "

"Maybe there's more to him than meets the eye! Still waters, and all that."

"Still waters, yes. He tends to keep himself to himself at class. Funny he knew Gabrielle and never said?"

"We're assuming he's a regular at the Workshops. Maybe this was his first visit."

"I wonder ..."

And they had a lot to think about as they went in and greeted their three deliriously happy canines and one aloof feline, tail a-twitch.

Chapter 12

Tamsin's Sunday morning lie-in was interrupted by her phone beeping at her. Her patient dogs recognised their opportunity and went through their extensive, excited, morning greeting, running round the bed and jumping on and off it. Stretching luxuriously, and looking out of the window at the bleak wet day - the rain on the glass blurring the view into so many green and grey splodges - Tamsin got up and checked her phone. It was a text from Feargal that had dredged her from her sleep.

"Got that info you wanted on the brother. Call me."

When she eventually arrived downstairs, Emerald already had the kettle on. "I heard that you were awake," she smiled as Tamsin looked puzzled.

"Quiz's tail thumping the radiator, remember? Rings through all the pipes in the house!"

"Ah yes, I'd forgotten that that's her bush telegraph to the catering department! I don't notice it," she laughed. "Here, Feargal has something on the brother. He asked me to ring him." And she took her mug and went to let the dogs back in again from the garden, flipping her phone to speaker as she dialled.

"There is a brother alright," said Feargal, picking up quickly. "He lives out Redmarley direction. Into horses. He's got some outfit there - livery, I think. And he does a bit of jump-racing himself."

"That confirms what Sara said. So he's a little guy?"

"No, I don't believe so. Not from the photos I've seen. You're thinking of flat racers. Jump jockeys tend to be more normal-sized."

"Oh, ok. Go on."

"There's not a lot more. He lives a comfortable life: decent car, no form - police form, that is. Plenty of racing form!" he laughed drily.

"Haha! So there are pictures of him?"

"Yes, getting prizes at races, that kind of thing. I don't know what he'll be able to tell you."

"We'll have to see. Will he be racing today?"

"I checked - there aren't any meets today this end of the country. And he's not that famous, so probably doesn't travel too far. I've got his address here - I'll text it to you."

"Thanks Feargal - you're a real help!"

"You scratch my back ..." he laughed.

"Fair enough. I'll be back with more news when I have it. Meanwhile I have another task for you to research ..." and she told him what she'd learnt about the herbs.

"Yes, these kids'll smoke anything. And who knows where they end up. It could certainly be a gateway drug for a serious pusher. But the horse connection - now that's very interesting. Very interesting indeed. I'll check that out. Look - take care won't you? If there is a doping connection with this brother fellow, it could represent big money and he's not going to welcome you snooping around."

"That's true enough. Specially as he's involved in horse-racing himself - he has to appear squeaky clean I guess ... But we'll still go. Play dumb. Just see what we can sniff out without directly asking anything. We can say in all honesty that we just want to clear Emerald's name."

"Take care!" he said again, as he rang off.

Tamsin tapped the phone against her chin then turned to Emerald. "I think the surprise drop-in may be better. If we ring he may say no and we won't get to meet him."

"Ok," sighed Emerald. "And we're not going to reveal anything?"

"Nothing at all. We're just going as friends of his sister, wanting to convey our sorrow at what happened. That's natural enough. And we'll keep our antennae working!"

"Yep. We seem to learn an awful lot by just listening and - feeling!"

"We do. Let's go. Looks like the rain may let up a bit soon."

The van sploshed through the puddles, the windscreen wipers working hard, till they got across the M50 motorway, then the sky seemed to become a more even grey and the heavy rain softened to a steady drizzle.

It was clear from the moment they arrived that there was money here. "Those horses look expensive," said Tamsin as she drove her van up the long well-tended drive flanked by pristine paddocks and immaculate fencing.

"Even their blankets look expensive!" said Emerald. "Like the sort of waterproof duvet jackets that horsey people wear. Look, they've even got neck-warmers that go right up to their ears!"

"Moonbeam would like one of those!" laughed Tamsin, then nodded to the expensive car parked in an open barn and sighed. "Ready to look innocent and sad?"

"Ready!"

As they got out of the van, a lithe, dark young man came round the side of the house carrying a full haynet over his shoulder. He peered at the *Top Dogs* sign on the van, looked surprised and came over with a challenging expression, standing erect and unwelcoming.

"You must be Alphonse!" smiled Emerald, "You look so like Gabrielle."

"You knew my sister?"

"Yes, I was there ... shortly before she died." And Emerald explained who she was and introduced Tamsin. "We wanted to offer our condolences, and say how sorry we were about the whole awful thing."

"We were on our way to Hartpury and remembered that you were here. So we wanted to drop by.

Gabrielle used to spend weekends with you, didn't she?"

Alphonse made no sign of wanting to be friendly or to invite them in despite the rain dampening them all and glistening on his sleek black wavy hair. "So you were the one who left her alone when she needed help?" his face darkened. Emerald pulled her hood up over her head and hunched her shoulders inside her jacket.

"Emerald thought she'd left. She'd offered help already, several times ..." Tamsin put in, jumping to her friend's defence.

"Slipshod. I understand from the police she was alone, out on the fire escape on a cold night. My poor sister ..."

"We wanted to say how sorry we were .." Emerald looked as though she might start crying again.

"I can understand how upset you must be," said Tamsin firmly, "but it seems it was totally an accident. That's how I believe the police are viewing it," she lied.

"They may. And they tell me no blame can be apportioned to the café or the class she attended. But it seems to me that more care should have been taken."

"Emerald kept suggesting she should go home. I heard her myself. She couldn't *throw* her out!" protested Tamsin.

"She said she just wanted a breath of fresh air, and then she took her things and went out via the fire escape. I thought she wanted to leave quickly and that she'd gone home that way, rather than waiting for me to unlock the front door when we all leave together." Emerald said unhappily.

"You've said your piece," replied Alphonse bitterly. "I hope it makes you feel better. But it won't bring my lovely sister back!" and with a toss of his black hair he shouldered the haynet again, turned on his heel and went to one of the paddock gates.

The two women turned silently to the van and drove away.

"Well!" said Tamsin crossly, once they were well away from the house, heading south towards Hartpury to maintain their fiction. "What a nasty man!"

"Perhaps he really loved her, and is looking for someone to blame," said Emerald miserably.

"He's not going to blame *you!* Gabrielle was an adult, not a small child. She chose to leave that way. Let's go home."

"At least nothing was said about herbs or horses."

"Or mushrooms."

"I'm glad." Emerald hunched herself back into her seat, while Tamsin got the de-mister going full blast. "I wouldn't want to be on the wrong side of that man. He's sharp. He'd have been on to us!"

"In fact, we're none the wiser, except that we know Alphonse is rich and unpleasant. I wonder what Feargal will unearth about these herbs. I do think there's a link here. Otherwise why would anyone want Gabrielle dead? She was such an innocuous person from all accounts."

"And either one or two people wanted her out of the way. I wonder if we can learn more from the health shop?"

"We'll go there again tomorrow. We've still got Alice and Jane to see."

"And the mysterious Kurt. Remember what Cameron said?"

"I do indeed. Let's walk that way tomorrow, and see whether he can actually reach his flat from the alley."

"Good plan!"

And they headed back home where Emerald indulged in a long yoga practice and a bubble bath while Tamsin opted for a damp dog walk on the Common to restore her equilibrium. Feeling cleansed after the meeting with Gabrielle's unpleasant brother, they met again afterwards for some soothing toast and honey in front of the gas fire, as the rain eventually stopped and the sky cleared, promising a frost the next morning.

Chapter 13

Monday was always busy for Tamsin, with home visits all day and a class in the evening. She still took time out to play with her dogs, and enjoyed working with Banjo and his new puzzle. He had to open the 'doors' of his toy in the right order to reveal the treat within. It was impressive how quickly he'd cracked the three-door puzzle, and now they were working on four doors.

Emerald also was out doing one-to-one yoga sessions about town, and they were to meet that afternoon at Jane's house, where they'd arranged to visit the two friends, Jane and Alice.

It seemed that these two spent a lot of time in each others' houses and Tamsin envied them their apparently simple and undemanding life. But only for a moment! She enjoyed her work, enjoyed being busy, enjoyed contributing to the world, not just taking from it - as so many people seemed to be content with doing. She'd rather work hard any day of the week than have oceans of free time to sit about chatting!

She was waiting in the van a little way down the road when Emerald arrived, swinging along fluidly, her yoga bag over her shoulder. "Here, stow that in the car," she called as she got out, and they walked down the road to no.94, which was almost identical to numbers 92 and 96 either side of it, and indeed all the other houses in the quiet residential road at the bottom of Malvern Link. Some residents had chosen different window designs, and a few had painted their front doors, in an attempt to stand out. But most of the differences were in the small front gardens, some spruce and well-tended, others neglected and with straggly hedging, and some with no garden at all - rather the whole front area had been paved and turned into a car parking area.

Jane's front garden was neat, sporting several pots of plants which now looked forlorn and untidy as the winter approached. The gravel drive was occupied by a small cheap car - a runabout, as people liked to call them.

Jane and Alice were all of a-flutter when they opened the door, together. Flushed and excited by their teacher's visit, their words tumbled out as they invited them into the sitting room where a laden tea tray awaited them on the coffee table. There was a three-piece suite covered with floral fabric with lots of ruffles and tassels, and the chairs all faced a large television set over a mantelpiece beset with vases and china figurines of shepherdesses and whimsical children, a carriage clock taking the centre place. A stack of romantic novels sat on a little reproduction table between the armchairs, and there were several magazines about celebrities and the royal family in a magazine rack next to the sofa. A magazine rack! Tamsin wondered how long it had been since she'd seen one of those! Must be twenty years, at least, she mused.

"You will have a cuppa?" asked Jane earnestly.

"And there's cake!" added Alice, passing round plates and dishing out tiny helpings of a dull-looking shop-bought cake.

It took a while to get settled with their tea and calm the friends down enough to focus them on the purpose of the visit.

"Ooh, isn't it awful!" they twittered. "Simply dreadful." "Such a lovely young girl!" and after several such comments, Jane added, "I reckon Harry's pretty put out about it."

"Harry?" echoed Tamsin.

"He had a thing for Gabrielle - didn't he, Alice."

"Quite a thing. I wondered if they'd become an item ..'

"But Gabrielle didn't seem interested."

"He did rather haunt her."

Tamsin asked, "Do you know if they met outside class?"

"Well," Alice leaned forward and spoke in a confidential voice, "I go to the health shop. There's a sort of tea they do that you can't get anywhere else - caffeine-free, you know - and I was there one day buying some, you see. I do like that tea, don't I, Jane? They've got such a big selection of teas and herbs there." Her double chin wobbled as she nodded vigorously, agreeing with herself.

Tamsin started to count to ten in her head. Despite her impatience she didn't want to interrupt this story.

"And I was just looking for the packet I wanted and the bell rang and in came Harry. I couldn't *see* him because I was in the second aisle along. You can't see the door from there. But I heard him alright."

"What did he say?" asked Emerald.

"He sounded quite menacing. And he said, uh, 'Have you made up your mind yet?' and Gabrielle said, um, something like," she imitated a girl's outraged voice "'I've told you Harry, I'm not doing this!'" .

"And did he see you, dear?" asked Jane, concerned.

"Not likely! Once I heard this was a kind of private conversation and he sounded so dangerous - not a bit like he usually sounds at all - I stayed very quiet and didn't move a muscle!"

Tamsin could just imagine this plump middle-aged lady cowering behind the tea display holding her breath, and had to suppress a giggle. "And what do you think he was referring to?"

"Absolutely no idea," Alice said with finality, carefully took another forkful of cake and sat back in her armchair.

"But they never appeared to know each other at class," said Jane, nodding her head fast. "Seems pretty fishy to me."

"So you're thinking they knew each other, had some dealings together, but weren't an item?"

"Definitely not an item. Seemed to be all one-way traffic there." Alice gave a knowing look.

Emerald asked, "How about that night. Did you see anything then? When we were leaving?"

But it seemed the two friends had been so busy chattering to each other on their way out that a coach and horses could have gone up the stairs past them and they wouldn't have noticed.

"They were very firm on pointing the finger at Harry," said Tamsin once they'd got back to the van. "Do you think they just don't like him?"

"Alice's story sounded true."

"It did. So what on earth had Harry wanted Gabrielle to do? And why so butch about it when he's normally such a caricature of a scatterbrained young man?"

"It could be to do with the herbs ... I do think they have something to do with it all. Do you think he was involved in pushing them?"

"I really can't imagine. It's dark already - let's go to the shop before it closes, then check out Kurt's route home. Do you know what he does?"

"Something to do with construction, I think. So he may be home fairly early, now it's getting dark. We can walk down the alley anyway and see if we can reach his place that way."

"Let's go!"

When they got to the shop they found Rose busy sweeping round the aisles. She looked quite put out by their arrival so near to closing time and she clearly hadn't acquired any social graces over the weekend. "Yeah?" she asked insolently.

"Just looking for some tea," said Tamsin.

Rose jerked her head towards the back of the shop, gave an exaggerated look at her wrist as if she wore a watch - though everyone her age used a phone - and with a loud sigh went back to her sweeping, as Tamsin located the tea at the back of the shop.

"Here's the tea - Emerald," she whispered. "you go over to the door and then to the counter. Say something too."

As she lurked in the tea aisle Tamsin could clearly hear Emerald asking what time they closed, and Rose's graceless response, "Five minutes, right?"

"Well, that confirms that Alice's story could be true," she said quietly as Emerald rejoined her. "There seems to be no loyalty to this shop from Rose. Let's see if she knows anything." They ambled down to the counter.

"Hey Rose, how's it going?"

Rose shrugged her shoulders. "It's a job, innit?"

"Bit different from most shops though. Bet you get some strange people in here!"

"You can say that again!" Having found an audience for her woes she leant on her broom and started in. "There was this woman come in - would only buy veg that arrived that morning. Weird." She warmed to her task, took a deep breath and carried on. "Then there was the one who reads *every word* on the label before she puts anything in her basket. Who does that?" She opened her mouth in a big O of astonishment and made a token sweep with her broom. "As for that other one, she asked me all these questions - I hadn't a clue. In the end she flounced out without buying a thing …"

"Do you ever get men shopping here?" Tamsin interrupted her flow of grievances.

"Nah. There's that old geezer who comes in every morning for coffee and a scone. Always has to have apricot jam with it. 'You haff the apricot yam, ya?' he says. Foreign." Tamsin smiled at the Worcestershire version of a German accent. Rose paused and gazed across to the till. "Hang on though. There was that bloke who came in - my first day. Young bloke. Only knocked over that display over there. Made an awful mess. He wanted Barry but he were out, weren't he." She shook her head. "Nah, hardly any men. Look, you gonna buy anything? I got to lock up now." She waved her wrist at them.

"Er yes, sorry - can I have these?" said Emerald, grabbing a bag of dried fruit and nuts from the counter. The purchase made, they thanked their new friend Rose with big smiles, and left.

"So Harry knows Barry," said Tamsin as they walked towards The Cake Stop.

"We don't know it was Harry. But there can't be many young men who are that clumsy!"

"Let's assume it was him for the moment. What does he do for a living?"

"I believe he works for Prenderghast's, the insurance people."

"Doesn't earn a lot then."

"I see what you mean. Yes, he could be open to a bit of private enterprise on the side."

"So he can drive that fast car of his. He must be getting money somewhere. We need to find a link between him and this herb business. If he's pushing hard drugs he may be in cahoots with Barry and his herbs. I wonder if Feargal can dig something out about that?"

They had passed the front door of the café and cut down the alley beside it. It was already dark, and they noted that the lights didn't automatically turn on as they passed the back entrance of The Cake Stop, and they could just make out the reflected light from the café on the metal railings of the fire escape, otherwise hidden in the gloom. They continued along the lane, reading the occasional faded house name or number on the rear gates of the houses in Plowman Street. Some of the gates had clear tracks worn in the hard ground, leading through to the gardens. Others were overgrown with elder and other wild plants. And as they plodded along the dark and scruffy lane, they came to no.37. This gate appeared to be padlocked shut, the grass and weeds growing happily against it. There was no worn track.

"Doesn't look like he gets home this way," said Tamsin.

They nodded sagely to each other, then Emerald pointed to a flattened clump of grass. "There are some broken stems here, so possibly he does come this way from time to time?"

They turned thoughtfully back down the alley as Tamsin said, "I have to whizz home and get my gear ready for my Trotley class. Let's get back to the car. We can talk more tonight. Perhaps we can talk to Kurt tomorrow before your class begins?"

Chapter 14

It was Tuesday, just a week since Gabrielle's death, and they were only visiting the last of the students today. Between their own busy schedules and actually finding times when the people would be in, it had taken them a whole week. Doubtless the police were well ahead of them, but they had heard nothing about any developments - even with Feargal having a mole in the station!

Today they were visiting West Malvern, to visit Linda the elderly ex-ballet-dancer, and Andrew, the young sports enthusiast. They couldn't be more different yet surprisingly they lived in the same house. Andrew rented a room from Linda, to help eke out her pension. They were uncomplicated people and the arrangement suited both of them.

As Tamsin and Emerald arrived up the narrow road the sun was setting and the sky still streaked with the leftover clouds from the heavy rain on Sunday. So they paused to admire the magnificent sunset - something they never got to see on their side of the ancient Hills.

As with so many of the houses plastered up the western slopes of the Malvern Hills, there were large picture windows affording a splendid view of the darkening hills over towards Wales, now burnished with the sunset glow. In Linda's case, these were French windows looking out onto the top shelf of her many-layered garden. A typical West Malvern garden cascading in steps down the steep hillside.

"You need to be fit to manage this garden, I'll bet!" said Tamsin, after spending some time admiring the view.

"You do indeed," agreed Linda, lithe and fit in the teeth of her years. "That's one reason Andrew came here. Oh, I hear him coming down the stairs now."

"I love gardens, and on my salary there was no hope of me acquiring one," he smiled as he strode into the room, hand outstretched in greeting.

"And I needed a bit of company to keep me human! I'm short of things to do since I retired from teaching dance. This is a marriage made in Heaven. Andrew does all the heavy work, and I tend the plants and tell him what to do," laughed Linda.

Tamsin and Emerald both relaxed in the easy presence of these two. Linda didn't feel any social pressure to provide them with refreshment and they were all happy to stay near the windows as the sun gradually sank from view, making a fantastic display of reds, oranges, and violets on the jagged clouds filling the sky.

"This is wonderful!" said Emerald as she gazed at the display. "You see this all the time?"

"Well not all the time," said Andrew, "but Mother Nature does a pretty good job of keeping us entertained. Sometimes I watch the sunset for so long that when I turn back into the room it appears pitch black. Time has moved on while I was caught up in the beauty."

"Talking of beauty," said Linda, "is there any news about poor Gabrielle? The police have been round here grilling us, but neither of us really had anything to offer."

"Not really any news, except that it may not have been an accident."

"*No!*" Andrew and Linda gasped in unison.

"Emerald's already feeling terrible about the whole thing - and it's affecting her livelihood. So we're trying to find out if anyone saw anything. Anything that could point to how it happened. How she fell."

"And why," added Emerald.

"All I can say is what I told that Inspector Hawkins," said Linda thoughtfully. "That Gabrielle was clearly unwell from the moment she arrived. But she wouldn't go home despite Emerald continually suggesting it. I heard you say it several times, dear. Then she grabbed her things and scooted out onto the fire escape as we finished our *Shavasana*."

"I thought she was going to be sick and urgently needed some fresh air," Andrew added.

"Then we all followed Emerald down to the front door as usual. I didn't see anything remarkable, did you?"

"No, nothing unusual," Andrew chewed his lip pensively.

"Did you see anyone go back into the room?" asked Tamsin.

Linda and Andrew looked at each other and shook their heads. "Nope," said Andrew, "we didn't. We were at the front of everyone going down the stairs.

Except for the little boy, who was jumping about - he's like me, the yoga energises him, rather than tiring him out."

"Oh, you're just full of energy the whole time!" laughed Linda. "I was like that, back in the day," she sighed.

Andrew's fresh boyish face, his freckled nose and his scruffy red hair were a picture of health and youthful enthusiasm as he smiled back at his friend.

"When he's not working he's never still," Linda explained. "Orienteering, mountain biking, yoga, gardening ..."

"Tennis and cricket too, don't forget!" he beamed.

"What's the day-job?" asked Tamsin.

"Accounting. Yes, I know, deadly dull, but it works for now. I'd really like to start some kind of open-air business, but haven't worked out what yet. I'd love to be able to give people a taste of the outdoors, provide rock-climbing and cycling and whatnot." He spoke with enthusiasm, a faraway look in his eye.

"That sounds amazing!" said Tamsin. Then, steering the conversation back to the subject that interested them most, "What did you make of

Gabrielle? Did she have any special friends, do you know? What were her interests?"

"She seemed a very nice young girl. Serious," said Linda. "She didn't have a boyfriend as far as I know."

"Harry had a bit of a thing for her - always mooning round her," added Andrew, "but I don't think she was interested. Didn't she work in the health shop?"

They were clearly not going to learn much more here, so they fell to chatting about the mountains they could just still see in the afternoon gloom, with Linda and Andrew both keen to point out the Black Mountains in the far distance, and Bromyard Downs rather nearer, over to the right. They were like a couple of happy birds, enjoying their surroundings so very much.

"I believe Sara's coming to class this evening," said Emerald airily as she headed to the front door.

Andrew's face transformed, "Really?" he said, looking like the cat who'd got the cream. "Jolly good! We'll see you later then."

Tamsin said quietly as they walked back up the steps to the road, "That's two definites for tonight then!"

"Let's make it three by bearding Kurt in his den."

Kurt answered the door when they arrived at the front of his house about fifteen minutes later. Such a large man, he completely filled the space of the doorway, looking quite daunting.

"Oh," he said. "It's you." Then he peered past Emerald at Tamsin and scowled.

"This is my friend Tamsin," Emerald beamed. Kurt stood back and gestured them to come in. "We were hoping to catch you," smiled Tamsin as she shuffled sideways past the large man in the narrow, musty-smelling, corridor - "Emerald's so anxious about this awful thing, and we wondered if you had any ideas about it."

"Why would I?" he asked abruptly.

"Ah, well, um, no reason really," stammered Emerald.

"We just wondered if you knew Gabrielle at all. Outside class, you know?"

Kurt's face melted for a moment at the mention of Gabrielle, then relapsed into its usual hard lines again. He chewed his lip pensively.

At that moment a magnificent long-haired cat strutted into the room yowling, tail held high. "Oh, what a lovely cat! She's the same colour as my Opal!"

Kurt's face softened again as he admired his beautiful cat.

"What's her name?" asked Tamsin, spotting the chink in the big man's armour.

"That's Candy," he said gruffly. Candy jumped lightly onto his lap and began purring as his huge calloused hands stroked her.

"She's beautiful!" they exclaimed.

"Gabrielle thought so too."

"Gabrielle came here?" asked Tamsin.

"No. No, I showed her a picture. On my phone, you know."

"Ah. Was that at class?" asked Emerald.

"Er no. I .." Kurt speeded up the cat-stroking in his confusion. "Saw her at a talk once, didn't I."

"Oh, that's nice! What was the talk about? They have such a lot of interesting talks round here," chattered Tamsin.

"Finding things to eat. Wild things. Free food - from the countryside. That kind of thing."

"How very interesting! Are you an expert in that?"

Kurt blushed slightly as he said, "Oh no. But I'm learning a lot. I just like to fend for myself, see. And Gabrielle. Well, she was all into natural stuff, weren't she. The health shop and that."

"Yes, so I believe. So … did you learn about what berries are safe to eat?" asked Emerald.

"And how to skin a rabbit?" added Tamsin.

"And how to tell mushrooms from toadstools?"

"Yer." The big man's face lighted up. "I were good at that one. Can tell my mushrooms, I can." Kurt smiled a little. "I showed Gabrielle some once, in the shop, like."

"When was that?" Tamsin couldn't help asking, then smiled to soften the question.

"Ooh, now yer asking. Must have been at the start of the season - couple of months ago, I'd say. Yer. That were it. Good while ago. Wanted to check they was the right ones."

"And they were?"

"Yer. Her said they were, and put them in her sandwich. In her sandwich!" he laughed raucously at this marvel, then fell to stroking the cat again. "I can teach you which ones to eat, if you want?"

"That's really kind of you, Kurt," said Tamsin. "And tell me, did you see Gabrielle that last evening - at class?"

"No more'n anyone else did," he said defensively.

"We're just trying to find out what happened, you see. And anyone may have seen something. Maybe just a little tiny thing, but it might give us some inkling of how she fell. I mean - maybe she jumped! What do you think, Kurt?"

"Oh no, she were too lovely to jump. No. Can't be that."

"Did you see her after class?" Emerald asked quietly.

"No, she left by the fire escape. I saw that."

"But you have a quick way of getting home don't you? Through the alley?" Tamsin tried.

"Oh yer. I do do that betimes. Nip home the back way," He grinned, showing gaps between his mis-shapen, slightly brown, teeth.

"So you'd have seen her, up on the fire escape."

"Nope." He spoke firmly then shut his mouth, and resumed stroking Candy, whose motor started up again loudly. "Pitch black it be, that alley. I knows the way, knows where the bins are, so I can walk back in the dark. Didn't see nothing at the back of the café. All dark, you see. Didn't see nothing," he nodded in emphasis.

"Got it."

"It's getting dark now," Emerald said, jumping up. "I have to go and get class ready! Will we see you there later, Kurt?"

"Oh yer. I'll be there." His face softened as he very gently placed the dozy cat on the sofa beside him, and got up to take them to the door. "Sorry I can't help you - over Gabrielle, you know. But I does miss her, I must say …"

"Well!" said Tamsin excitedly as they regained the street. "What do you make of that!"

"Maybe the mushroom mystery is solved," said Emerald.

"I'm not so sure. He may appear simple, but did you notice how neat and tidy his flat is? I'd say if he says he knows mushrooms, then he knows mushrooms."

"Deliberate?" Emerald turned to look at her.

"Dunno. He seems a bit soft on her. Could be a controlling thing? The only way he could control this beautiful creature?"

"Pretty weird, I'd say." Emerald hunched her shoulders up inside her coat. "But actually, I need to rush. Let me get my things from your van."

"Tell you what. You go ahead and join your people in The Cake Stop. They like that, and they'll be needing reassurance. I'll fetch your things over to you there. See you in a mo." And Tamsin peeled off to find her van.

Chapter 15

By the time Tamsin arrived in The Cake Stop, Emerald was happily chatting with her slightly diminished flock. Looking around, Tamsin could see that Harry was not there - as he'd threatened. He probably would never come again. Nor was Saffron there. Perhaps her baby is fretting, she thought, not wanting to imagine that everyone was deserting her friend.

She took her coffee over and shuffled onto the bench beside Cameron and Molly. Young Cameron as ever was full of energy and excitement for life.

"You're an inspiration, Cameron, so you are!" she grinned at him.

Cameron looked blankly at her till Molly jogged his elbow and he said, "Thank you," smiled, and wondered what he'd owned up to.

Now Tamsin could see that Shirley was also missing. Wonder what's up with that? Linda and Andrew were there, and Andrew sprang to life as the big main door opened and in came Julia and Sara. He fussed around them equally, but had eyes only for Sara, who was friendly enough without being hugely encouraging. Andrew definitely looked the "lovesick puppy" that Sara had suggested he was, but Tamsin knew that capable Sara was flattered by his attentions, and she could see that she clearly enjoyed his company, laughing happily as they talked together. And that furthermore she was effectively being chaperoned by her lift, Julia, so she had nothing to fear.

While Tamsin was chatting with them about how Sara's mare Crystal was doing at her college, and life in the Bishop's Green Cottages, Jane and Alice arrived giggling, with rosy cheeks and clear excitement. Had they had a tipple before they came, Tamsin asked herself, or were they just enthralled by the whole affair? Kurt had slipped in and taken up his station at the foot of the stairs. Never one for mixing, Kurt. His attempts to befriend Gabrielle had hinged on their common interest. Or was he only interested in foraging because she had been?

Emerald took her yoga bag from Tamsin and shepherded her flock towards the upper room, and Kylie swooped on their abandoned tables to clear up.

"Now I can have some cake at last!" said Tamsin, passing some mugs over to Kylie, who said, "I'll bring it over. Give me your card. What would you like?" Tamsin leaned back in her chair to peer at the cake cabinets and said, "You choose! Give me something I'll love!"

And a few minutes later while she was checking her phone messages, a wet nose pressed itself into her leg.

"Muffin!" she exclaimed, and looking up saw Charity bearing a tray.

"I've brought you your cake, dear, and your card. Kylie said to be sure I gave that back to you. No dog?"

"Thank you! Here, sit down," said Tamsin, clearing table space for the tray, by now with Muffin on her lap. "Evening Muffin - mine are all at home. What's the news?"

"I should be asking you that question!" I know you've been sleuthing all over the place."

"How do you know that?" Tamsin was concerned.

"Well, I don't really. Except I know you. And don't tell me you're not doing your best to beat the police at their own game again."

"You got me," laughed Tamsin as she took a large spoonful of lemon meringue pie. "Mmmm," she said, her eyes glazing over with the intense flavour and the sugar rush.

"We've learnt some interesting things, as a matter of fact. But you have to keep all this under your hat, Charity," she said quietly in the gradually-emptying café.

"I will. I do realise there could be danger. I'm not going to send any trouble your way. I'd hate to think of you walking into a trap, like I did!"

Tamsin shuddered at the memory of when she had nearly lost her old friend. "Well, it's like this ..." and Tamsin told her about all their visits, and the stand-out points they'd learnt. About Harry being very interested in Gabrielle, and going back up to the upper room that night. About the special herbs in Barry's health shop as possible lead-in to harder drugs. The horse connection through Alphonse.

Harry's nasty remarks to Gabrielle. Kurt's mushroom interest, and him not seeing Gabrielle from the alley. She tossed in that Andrew was soft on Sara, as Charity was very fond of her too, since the girl had literally galloped to her rescue that time. "He has that nice Linda keeping him on the straight and narrow," she added.

"I don't know why Shirley is missing today. She hadn't sent a message to Emerald."

"Just reverting to type, I expect. When trouble looms she's always kept her head down."

"True. Though she was really coming out of her shell when we spoke to her last week. Harry isn't here, but he told us he wouldn't be. I suspect that now Gabrielle's gone he has no need to be here."

"What sort of connection did they have exactly?"

"I think maybe Harry was involved with the herbs and getting kids onto something harder. I have no proof - it just seems to point that way. And he was very resistant and pretty off-hand when we visited him. I don't think he's what he seems ..."

"If he's pushing drugs he should be well off. Any sign of that?"

"The house looked very much a rented soulless place with an unkempt garden. He seems to have little interest in his surroundings. But there was an expensive car there, you're right. I'm no good at cars, but Feargal reckoned from what I told him that it was some sort of boy-racer Merc."

"What does he do for a living? I mean, officially."

"Something to do with insurance. He works for Prenderghast's."

"Don't they have that poky little office over the second-hand bookshop? He shouldn't be able to afford a fast car, then," Charity said with finality, as she twirled Muffin's ear, its owner being now firmly ensconced back on her owner's lap.

"And if he's involved in sales he's presumably able to go all over the place all the time, on the road - plenty of opportunity." Tamsin took the last spoonful of the lemon meringue pie and savoured it. "The thing is, we've learnt a lot, but we're no further forward. In terms of proof, I mean. Lots of conjecture - nothing solid."

They both sat back for a few moments, thinking.

"Tell me more about Kurt and these mushrooms," said Charity quietly, nodding her head towards the stairs to the upper room where Emerald's class was going on.

"Well, it seems he may have had a crush on Gabrielle, and possibly took an interest in foraging to get closer to her. He took some of his finds to her to check he had the right ones, but he said it wasn't last week - rather it was months ago. She assured him they were good and took some for her lunch. He seems a simple soul at heart. Simple in mind too. But he can't seriously have thought that the lovely young dark beauty Gabrielle could have been interested in him romantically?"

"I wonder just how simple he is ..." mused Charity. "I don't mean that he deliberately set out to kill her. But there has to be a connection there with the poisoning. Maybe he made a mistake over mushrooms and doesn't want to own up to it?"

"Or maybe he did it deliberately? But why on earth would he do that, if he was sweet on her?"

Their questions were destined to stay rhetorical, as the figure of Jean-Philippe loomed over their table.

"*Bonsoir, mesdames!*" he said chirpily. "I see I'm interrupting a pow-wow. Has the Malvern Hills Detective solved the mystery yet? Inspector Hawkins certainly hasn't. It seems they're accepting it as an accident." He pulled forward a chair and sat down.

"They don't appear to have got any further forward," Charity nodded.

"But then neither have we!" said Tamsin with annoyance.

"We know Gabrielle had already been poisoned, and we know the fall was no accident - sorry, can't say how we know," she held up her hand to forestall the question forming on Jean-Philippe's lips, "sworn to secrecy I'm afraid. But it's true."

"But we don't know if one person or two were involved," Charity put in.

"Though we are getting closer to who *may* have done it, and importantly - why."

"You losing your touch?" said Jean-Philippe with a crooked smile, and his characteristic Gallic bushy-eyebrow-raise.

Tamsin made a mock-angry face then grinned. "Last time - last two times, in fact - something else happened which made it clear who had done what. I wonder if that may happen this time?"

"It would be a great help if it did," said Charity, "though it didn't seem like it at the time." She shivered.

"You think someone else is *en danger*?"

"I think the stakes may be high enough for that to be so ... Oh, I wish I could see more clearly!" She reached out for Muffin. "I'll have to ask the dogs, won't I, Muffs? They may have some ideas. I hope so, as I'm clean out of them."

And so saying, they noticed the empty tables all around them and got up to leave.

Chapter 16

"Whatcher doing?" asked Emerald as she floated down the stairs the next morning, accompanied as ever by the dot-dot-dot of Opal descending ahead of her.

"There you go, Banjo - that was great!" Tamsin got up from the floor and brushed the dusty knees of her trousers with her hand. "One day I'll be able to afford a cleaner for this place," she smiled, picking up Banjo's puzzle. Quiz greeted Emerald with a languid tail-wave, while Moonbeam stuck her nose in Opal's ear and sniffed noisily till the cat batted her on the muzzle with her sheathed claws and, tail raised, strutted to the kitchen where she expected her breakfast to be served.

"How's Banjo's puzzle going?" Emerald did her duty by her cat first before filling the kettle.

"He's amazing! I was watching him think. You can see how he looks at one door, then another, makes his decision and goes for it."

"That's amazing that he can pull back and think it out like that. You kind of expect dogs to just rush in. Not sit back and work it out."

"You've done it again." Tamsin leant against the worktop and folded her arms across her chest.

"Made you coffee?" grinned Emerald.

"No, silly. Hit the nail on the head. You always do it. I don't know why I can't see these things ..."

"How do you mean?" Emerald opened the fridge for the milk.

"I've been going at this puzzle head on. I haven't been looking at the nuances, the stories within the stories. I need to step back and take a clearer view." She took a sprig of grapes, picked one off and started to munch on it. "I think there are a lot of threads to this affair. Not as clear-cut as I initially thought."

"Do you mean the mushrooms and the push were done by different people?"

"I think so now, yes." She waved the hand holding the grapes then bent to scoop up the one she'd just dropped as the three dogs stared at it, waiting to see if they'd be allowed to have it. "No sorry, dogs, you can't eat grapes - they'll kill you. The poisoning has to be Kurt. God knows why. Could still be an accident. If he was sweet on her I can't imagine why he'd want to kill her. But I think the inner workings of Kurt's mind are probably a bit of a mystery."

"And the push is from a nastier person. That was really horrid."

"Exactly. Two different people. If Kurt had poisoned her on purpose, he wouldn't need to kill her. He could just wait."

"Kurt is not the sharpest knife .."

"That's putting it mildly. I'd say 'special needs' at least."

".. so maybe we should talk to him again?"

"I think so. But I'm going to do it in the open, or at least have Feargal with me! Charity was reminding me last night about not putting myself in a vulnerable position. Even if I trusted Kurt ... which I don't."

"I've got this retreat coming up on Friday - you remember, don't you? - the weekend thing I told you about? I've been so looking forward to it ... I'm glad you talked me out of cancelling! So I've packed loads of sessions in today and tomorrow."

"That's ok." She put a comforting hand on Emerald's arm. "You need to be out of this for a couple of days. It's been very hard on you. I'll give Feargal a shout."

"He should have news for us anyway - it's been days since we last heard from him. I have to rush. See you later!" And so saying, she took her mug and headed back up the stairs to get her kit ready for her first session, leaving Tamsin to ponder what she'd just been thinking.

And when she rang Feargal later she got through to him immediately. They agreed to meet to catch up, and Feargal was keen to accompany her on this latest mission.

"How are we going to catch him, out of his flat?"

"I think if we hang around near there at the same time as we went yesterday there's a good chance of catching him. We could head over to the Priory Gardens and get him talking about plants and things."

"Plants and things?"

"Oh, there's a lot for you to catch up on! See you later."

Naturally, the Cake Stop had been chosen as their meeting-place. "You deal with that first," said Tamsin, as she ogled the enormous slice of carrot cake Feargal had brought to the table for himself.

"Want some?" he asked, noticing her fixation.

"No! No, I'm being good today." She eyed the succulent icing, swallowed and said, "Eat it quickly please!"

"Ok. Well I haven't found out too much to be honest. I've been working at it a lot. It's awful that this happened to Emerald." His expression became slightly misty as he said her name. "We have to get this resolved *asap*! So .. Alphonse seems to lead a fairly blameless life. No huge spending - though he deals in quite large sums in his business. It's not cheap, the service he provides." He shovelled a large forkful of cake in and mumbled through the crumbs, "Harry is known to the police. All fairly small-scale stuff. But he's one of those people they keep an eye on. In case he moves up the food chain a bit."

"That doesn't surprise me. Not an attractive person, I'd say. Is clumsiness a symptom of drug abuse?"

"Clumsiness, lack of co-ordination, irritability …"

"That fits the bill. He certainly got irritable with Gabrielle," and she told Feargal the story.

"So that's one definite line of enquiry," he said, as he pushed his plate away and licked his fingers. "What's all this about Kurt and plants?"

Tamsin leaned across the table and said quietly, "He's into mushrooms. He's been to the same foraging classes that Gabrielle was at. Don't know if that was coincidence or he was stalking her. But he's proud of knowing his fungi. Seems he compared notes with Gabrielle when he first started picking mushrooms."

"Fishy. Definitely. Good lead!"

"Yup. And I think we ought to question him more closely. Emerald's off on some yogic retreat for a couple of days - she needs the break - and I don't want to talk to him alone. Makes me nervous!"

"And you want me to weigh in?"

"'Yer', as Kurt would say. He's a big guy. Thought outdoors would be safest, and with a bit of back-up."

Feargal spread his arms to demonstrate his slender form, and smiled.

"Yes, you're not brawny, but .. brainy!" laughed Tamsin. "And male," she added. "I don't want to go to his flat again, anyway. So I thought we could hang about near his front door and intercept him there."

They settled back to enjoy their coffees while they waited for the clock to tick its way round to Kurt's likely homecoming time. While Tamsin missed having a dog to distract her, Feargal fidgeted and fiddled with his phone.

"Here! Get this!" he jumped forward with enthusiasm. "You know Shirley Vaughan? You wondered why she wasn't here for class yesterday, didn't you say?"

"Yeah?" encouraged Tamsin. "Is this something from your mole?"

"My lips are sealed," Feargal smiled smugly, but his eyes sparkled. "She's only spent the night in A & E."

Tamsin gaped. "What happened?"

Feargal was scanning his phone rapidly. "Dunno. Just that she was admitted last night with a stab-wound and kept in overnight."

"*Stab-wound!* Who stabbed her?"

"She won't talk. Insisted on that wastrel son of hers - Mark, isn't it? - being summoned to her bedside. She was pretty woozy from whatever they gave her, so the police are going round again today. What on earth can Shirley have to do with this?"

"You think it's connected?"

"You don't?"

"You're right. Too much of a coincidence. This thing has tentacles. It's a bit worrying. I wonder if Emerald is safe, with her class? Can you let me know what you discover later?"

"Sure. Time to move off now, and have a go at Kurt."

Chapter 17

As they left the Cake Stop, returning the cheery waves from Jean-Philippe and Kylie, they found themselves face to face - almost bosom to bosom - with the two excited middle-aged friends from the yoga class.

"My dear!" squeaked Jane, in high excitement.

"Just the person!" echoed Alice, pressing forward, and eying Feargal with a sparkle in her eye and a sickly grin.

"You won't believe it! I'm so glad we've run into you." said Jane.

"We've got *information!*" added Alice.

"For Emerald really. But you'll do nicely instead," Jane continued.

Alice stared boldly at Feargal and simpered, "Aren't you going to introduce us to your young man?"

Jane nudged her friend with her elbow, as Tamsin stammered, "Oh this is a friend of ours. He's keen to help Emerald too .."

"Oh, that's alright then," beamed Jane, who appeared to be the ring-leader.

"So what's this information?" asked Feargal letting his red hair flop over his brow, working hard to look as handsome as possible.

This sent both ladies into a flutter, until Jane said, "Well ..."

They waited.

"Well. We were walking to the shopping centre - you know the one with the big supermarket?"

"We needed some biscuits, you see," added Alice helpfully.

"And as we passed the end of the big Council estate, who should *race* past us, but ..."

Tamsin and Feargal had decided with a glance that the only way to hear this story was to allow the ladies their moment of glory and wait them out.

"Who?" Tamsin encouraged, looking as interested as she could.

"Harry!" They chorused.

"Where was he going?"

"I'm not sure he knew! Only a couple of moments later another young man came hurtling out of the estate and flew after him."

"It was *so* exciting," gasped Jane.

"Just like something out of a film!" said Alice.

"So where did they go?"

The two women turned and looked at each other in bafflement.

"What do you think, dear?" asked Jane.

"I didn't see," wailed Alice. "They'd run past the end of our road, you see."

"What time was this?" asked Feargal.

Alice looked appreciatively at him, convinced he must in fact be Tamsin's beau. "Oh - now *that* I can tell you!"

"Yes, we know what time it was."

Tamsin kept her impatience in check.

Alice began, "We'd just watched the antiques show - you know, the one with that nice man who always wears such dapper suits .."

"He's quite a card!" interjected Jane. "Do you remember that time they found the silver salver ..."

"What time does the antiques show end?" interrupted Feargal.

"Oh, it finishes just before five, of course. Just gives us time to run out for anything we need before our soaps start at 6.30!"

"We love the soaps, don't we Alice! Which ones do you like, dear?"

Tamsin smiled and said, "Actually I'm usually teaching at that time," and hoped she'd wriggled out of the question successfully.

"In fact, hadn't you better get moving? You don't want to miss anything," said Feargal, grabbing his moment. Tamsin pulled her hood up against the fine drizzle that had just begun.

So they said their goodbyes and left the two ladies chirruping to each other on the pavement.

"We'd better run so we don't miss our quarry," said Feargal urgently, as he pulled a tiny folding umbrella from his Barbour jacket's deep pocket and put it up against the rain, which had turned from drizzle to cold raindrops very quickly.

They did hurry. But after waiting for three-quarters of an hour opposite Kurt's flat, where they could see the dark windows and an occasional glimpse of Candy the cream cat on the window-ledge inside, they decided they'd had enough rain and damp for one day and headed for their respective homes.

But they had had time while they sheltered in a doorway to go over the latest developments in more detail. There was Shirley, in hospital with a stab-wound, her son at her side. There was Harry running fast through Malvern Link at a time when he should have been at his office in Great Malvern, or on the road selling insurance to someone.

"Wonder who the other young man was?"

"Could be anyone. Maybe someone Harry owed money to?"

"Maybe someone he'd sold bad stuff to?"

"Who do we know who could fit the bill?"

"Only Andrew." Tamsin scraped the ground with the toe of her boot.

"He's fit, and a runner."

"But fresh-faced and clean-living from what you told me."

"Not Andrew, I'm sure." She carried on making patterns in the wet pavement with her foot. "Mark!" she exclaimed, turning to face him. "What about him? Shirley's son. Bit of a wide boy himself - you remember! I wonder if this is something to do with the attack on her?"

"Perhaps it's Harry we should be interviewing. I'm happy to be there. I don't trust him at all from what I've heard. Don't think you should see him alone."

"He's a small-time weasel, I think. But who knows - maybe he killed Gabrielle! You're right. Do come with me. I keep thinking of what happened in the woods over the Trotley case - and poor Charity!"

"You're right - can't be too careful when dealing with homicidal maniacs," Feargal smiled sweetly. "Fill me in on what you know about this ne'er-do-well as we wander back."

So for the second time in as many days, Tamsin went over everything she knew. They tried to piece it together, but there were just too many holes.

"We need to find out more about what happened to Shirley."

"And what the connection is - if any - between Harry and Alphonse."

"How are you fixed tomorrow?" asked Feargal after they'd walked the few hundred yards back to their cars without seeming to get a single step further in the case.

"Free all morning - then jampacked the rest of the day till about 6."

"Good to hear the Malvern dogs are keeping you busy by misbehaving at every opportunity."

"It sure is! Bless them. If only people would realise that dogs are people too," she smiled broadly as she opened the door of her van and tossed her wet coat in, "but then I'd be out of business."

So they arranged to meet up the next morning near the bookshop, to go to Prenderghast's Insurance - Harry's place of work - to try and catch him.

Chapter 18

Next morning saw Tamsin and Feargal ascending the scruffy and worn sisal stair-carpet on the narrow staircase of the insurance office to talk to Harry again. Tamsin put her hand on the wooden hand-rail then rapidly removed it with a grimace. "Sticky!" She pulled a face. "We need to find out why he really ever went to the yoga classes. Clearly not his thing really."

"I think I'll lean on him a bit - suggest we know about his illegal activities," said Feargal, trudging up the narrow staircase behind her.

But when they arrived at the reception desk, the bored girl behind it paused the game she was playing on her phone and said, "Harry? Nah. Not been in today." Then she leaned forward, glancing furtively over to the main office behind the glass door, and spoke in her best confidential voice, "Mind you, I'm not surprised! With all the carry-on yesterday." She leant back in her chair again and started to swivel it from side to side as she waited for a reaction.

Feargal knew exactly what would work with this girl, and leant forward over the tall desk with a wink. "Tell all!" he whispered.

Delighted to have found an audience - and a handsome one at that - the girl started an animated rendition of the events of the previous evening.

"There's this woman, see?"

"What woman?" asked Tamsin.

"I dunno, do I?" came the scornful answer. Tamsin felt a nudge from Feargal's foot and shut her mouth again. Then, ignoring her entirely, the girl looked intently at Feargal and said, "This woman, see? She storms into the office - in there," she nodded to the glass door. "She clocked him through the glass - went straight past me without a by-your-leave - and starts yelling at Harry. *'You leave my son alone! I don't want you near him!'* She was in a right state. I got up, of course, and went to see what was going on. Had to, didn't I." She leaned forward again and hissed in a stage whisper, "She was only waving a knife in his face!"

Feargal looked suitably shocked. "She'd brought a knife?"

"Nah. It was the paperknife from off of Harry's desk. You know, for opening letters and that."

Feargal nodded and smiled encouragingly.

"So all the noise brought old man Prenderghast out of his office. He came rushing over and tried to quieten her down. She weren't having any of it and kept waving the knife at Harry."

"No!" said Feargal, the perfect audience.

"*Yeah!*" She nodded enthusiastically, smiled coyly, drew a deep breath and carried on, "And - just as Mr.Prenderghast told me to ring the police, the woman screamed *'You keep away from Mark!'* and ran out of the office, Harry right behind her. They clattered down those stairs and I could see him reaching out to grab her. She was still screaming something awful, and that was the last we saw of both of 'em."

She leant back triumphant and started swivelling her chair back and forth again.

"Amazing!" Tamsin tried to give her the response she deserved, but only got a dismissive look.

"So what happened to the knife? Did she leave it behind?"

"She only ran off with it, didn't she!"

"And there was a tussle on the stairs?"

"I said, didn't I." She began to look sullen. "That was before the ambulance came. But I had to deal with a customer, so I didn't see what was going on."

"Did you get to call the police? You'd make an excellent witness - you're super-observant!"

She fluttered her eyelashes and looked pleased. "Nah. Mr.P said don't bovver. Since they were both gone and didn't look like coming back."

"Well thank you - that's really helpful. Any idea if Harry *will* be coming back?"

"Not if he's got any sense. You should have heard the boss once he'd gone. 'When I think of what I've done for that good-for-nothing so-and-so!' he said. 'If he comes back, you can hand him a cardboard box and tell him to clear his desk,' he said. He'll ruin the good name of Prenderghast!'" She giggled. "He was ever so cross."

"I can understand that," agreed Feargal heartily. "Listen, you're a great help - see you around." He winked again and they left her blushing as they set off down the rickety stairs again.

"Well!" said Tamsin, once they were away from the office and stepping round the tables of second-hand books in front of the shop below.

"So it must have been Shirley."

"And that's how she got stabbed!"

"Kinda self-inflicted wound."

"Poor Shirley. She's normally so reserved and distant. I guess the Mama Bear came out when she found Mark was hanging about with Harry."

"And she can recognise a crook fast - with all Mark's poor choices."

"Wonder what they were up to?" mused Tamsin. "Think we should make a hospital visit to the sick?"

"Good idea. Time for some Christian charity, I think. Though she may clam up again."

"Worth a try, anyway. Hope she's not in intensive care. This evening? It's usually 6 or 7 or so, visiting hours, isn't it? I'll be through by then."

"I'll find out and let you know. We can meet there. Gotta go now, I'm afraid. What are you up to now? Don't you have to work for a living any more?"

Tamsin laughed. "I'm off to a home visit shortly, in Upton. I think I might drop in on Saffron first - she's just down the road from there. I have an itchy nose about her, and why she wasn't there on Tuesday. She never said anything to Emerald."

"You think something's up with her?"

"Let's say I just have a feeling. Unfinished business. Maybe something she said. Dunno."

It wasn't long till Tamsin's van pulled up outside Blossom Cottage. This time she was greeted with much yapping and leaping about from Napoleon who was keeping Saffron company in the front garden, where she was sweeping up leaves.

"Oh, you're better!" Tamsin grinned from ear to ear.

"Better?" Saffron straightened up and looked puzzled.

"You weren't there on Tuesday. Wondered if something was up. Charlie's ok, I hope?"

"Oh yes, he's fine. He's napping at the moment. It's getting a bit nippy out here - won't you come in?" And she scooped Napoleon up so that Tamsin could open the gate and come in. "Thing is, I was so exhausted on Tuesday after a night and a day of Charlie squawking that when he at last went to sleep I crashed out on the sofa. Sorry."

As they got inside to the kitchen, Saffron leant over the baby monitor for a moment to enjoy the silence, quietly closing the kitchen door to make sure nothing disturbed the infant. And while she cleared a space on the counter - cluttered with baby bottles and the ubiquitous nappy basket - to assemble coffee things, Tamsin idly gazed at the corkboard on the back of the kitchen door which had stayed open last time. There was the usual confusion of notes, reminders, receipts, bills, and also a couple of postcards, one with a picture of Cheltenham Racecourse and the words *Gold Cup!,* and the other from Aintree, home of the Grand National. Interesting, she thought, while some cogs in her mind slipped into place. Ah! That's it - that's what was nagging me. Tamsin set her lips together and mentally nodded. The baby has a definite Latin colouring. And who else had that colouring? Gabrielle and Alphonse! And Alphonse rode jump races ... It all started to slide together.

She didn't really need to talk to Saffron now. She knew. But why had Saffron claimed not to know Gabrielle, who was her child's aunt? She plonked herself down firmly at the little kitchen table and awaited her mug, realising that all this time Saffron had been talking about baby bottles and the trouble with trying to keep up her milk supply.

"Ah," she said, feeling a response was overdue. "Must be difficult, on your own." And receiving her mug with effusive thanks, she diverted the conversation to the view out of the window, and what a lovely little garden she had for young Charlie to explore once he got his legs under him.

"Yes, it is nice. And I'll want to get a sandpit and swings and all that for next summer, but," Saffron sighed, "I'll have to earn some money first." And she put on a brave smile as she looked back at Tamsin, who was quick to latch on to her suggestion that money was short to ask whether the absent father contributed to his child's care.

"He sends the odd cheque. When he thinks about it. But no, not really."

"Oh, that's awful. Does he see Charlie?"

"No. And as he walked out on me, I'm not really bothered. I mean, it's tough on Charlie, but," she held her chin up, "we'll manage. He doesn't need a father like that."

"So is Charlie's Dad not well off?"

"He's very well off. But he's got everything tied up in a limited company, so it looks as though he doesn't earn much. So they can't get him." She looked downcast.

"That sounds nasty. Surely you can get the Government to weigh in and help make him pay?"

"I believe I can, yes. But honestly, it's so tiring looking after a baby - specially one who doesn't want to sleep. I'm bone-tired … I have no idea when I'll be able to start my business again and actually earn some money," she sighed. "You're right though. I'll have to do something about it. Thanks for giving me a nudge!"

"I hate to see women being treated badly. It's just plain wrong. You could start with the Citizens' Advice Bureau - I'm sure they know all about this. Don't they have solicitors volunteering their services?"

"I believe that's so. Right! I'm going to do that tomorrow! I've been feeling sorry for myself - but no more. I'll go down there and see what can be done."

"Charlie deserves it," Tamsin said quietly, knowing that this would seal the deal.

"You know what? I've been feeling so down, fuzzy-headed from lack of sleep ... you're a real friend! You've let me see light at the end of the tunnel! Thanks, Tamsin - I won't forget this! And tell Emerald I'll be there next Tuesday."

She had trouble keeping her equilibrium on the way to her home visit once she left Saffron - she was so annoyed that Alphonse should go to such lengths to deprive his baby of his financial support. She and Emerald had taken an instant dislike to him - now they were utterly vindicated in their opinion.

But once she arrived at her appointment and met Willow, the 9-week-old chocolate brown Working Cocker Spaniel puppy she'd come to help with, it all evaporated from her mind as she enjoyed the little pup and relished doing what she did best.

Chapter 19

So Tamsin was feeling very happy with the world – an hour with a puppy always had that healing effect! – as she pulled into the car park at the big hardware store between Upton and home. The light bulb in the living room had died the night before, and extensive rummaging in the shed had failed to turn up the right sort of bulb to replace it. Whizzing in and scooping up a pack of bulbs, she saw in the queue ahead of her the large shape of Kurt. He was buying a couple of boxes of screws. She chewed her lip in thought for a moment, then reflected on how very busy the store and the car park were.

So she caught up with him as he was dropping the boxes onto his passenger seat.

"Hi Kurt! We meet again!" she said cheerily.

He gave her a lopsided gap-toothed smile, saying, "No Emerald today?"

"Ah no. Don't know what she's up to. I just dropped in for these," and she waved the box of light bulbs. "Tell me Kurt, I was wondering … how do you know which mushrooms are alright to eat? I see them on my dog walks, you see, and I don't dare pick any!" she lied.

Kurt looked pleased at being asked, and launched into a potted lecture about what to look for in a mushroom to know it was safe.

Tamsin frowned and nodded as he spoke, "That's really helpful! And I bet you compared notes with Gabrielle, as you had a common interest?"

"I gave Gabrielle some I'd found once."

"Oh yes, you said. That's nice!"

"Yer. I'd picked too many, so I dropped round to the shop with them. I'd do that sometimes. Slice them all up ready, like, so she could put them straight into her sandwich for lunch. Always had a lot of salad in her sandwich, did Gabrielle. Very healthy she was. You know, ate the right things." He nodded approvingly.

Tamsin hid her astonishment. "When did you do that? I mean was it just weekends when you'd go mushrooming?"

"Nah. I gets up early in my line of business." He pushed his shoulders back. "Tis the early bird gets the worm," he guffawed at his joke, showing that he was really a very simple fellow in a very large frame.

Tamsin laughed easily, "And it's the early forager who gets the best mushrooms!"

"Yer right there!" Kurt laughed loudly and relaxed a bit more. "Oh Lummy - there's my foreman. I'd best get going. Nice to meet you again Miss," he touched his forelock as he lumbered his great bulk into his car, leaving Tamsin clutching her light bulbs to her, mouth slightly open.

She checked the time as he drove off and saw she would just be able to fit in a very necessary and restorative dog walk on the Common before shooting off for her last two home visits of the day, then on to see Shirley in hospital.

So when she eventually fetched up at the hospital it was with a sigh of relief that she found a chair to fall into and wait for Feargal. He'd said he'd be there at ten to seven so they could discuss strategy. She stretched her tired legs out in front of her and closed her eyes for a moment. When she opened them again, she saw him striding through the glass double doors.

"Looks like we can visit any time," she nodded to the big notice as he landed in the chair next to hers.

"Hallo to you too," he smiled. "I know. But I thought there was a better chance of Mark having got fed up and gone out for the evening if we left it late."

"Ok. Well, here's what I learnt today. There's a very, *very* high chance that Saffron's baby is Alphonse's." Feargal's eyebrows shot up in surprise. "In which case, she lied to us about hardly knowing Gabrielle."

"Now, I wonder why?" Feargal flicked his red hair off his brow, his knee jiggling up and down as he sat beside her.

"Maybe just to distance herself from Gabrielle's death? Or maybe she just wants to distance herself from the whole family, given where it's landed her."

"Hmm. We need to know a bit more. Is Alphonse involved with the baby at all."

"Seems not. She's having difficulty pinning 'the father'" - she waved her hands in air-quotes -

"down for child support, as he's doing some creative accounting to hide his money."

"That's sick."

"Absolutely. I told her to go and get some free legal help. She needs to fix this. Other than that, I don't think she has anything to do with the murder. And it would be the brother she'd want to push off a fire escape, not Gabrielle!"

"So that's another one out. We're running out of suspects …"

"Not so fast! Listen to this! Guess who I ran into at the hardware store."

Feargal looked blank. "You know I hate guessing games."

"It was Kurt!"

"Hey, I thought you weren't going to talk to him on your own."

"The shop was busy, and so was the car park. Broad daylight. So I thought I'd give it a go," and with relish she told him about Kurt giving sliced-up mushrooms to Gabrielle to put in her lunch.

"How extraordinary," interjected Feargal. "Is this a strange Worcestershire courtship ritual?"

Tamsin smirked.

"Wow! So he likely fed her Death Cap. And we're going to find out whether it was deliberate or accidental, right? When did he last give her some?"

"I was about to ask him that when he saw his foreman and bolted. At least, that's what he said ... perhaps he's not as simple as he makes out?"

"Clearly another interview needed. And this time, don't do it alone. If he did poison Gabrielle, he's clearly nuts. I mean, how many people know about these fungi, and were connected with her? The finger will point straight at him. He can't be that stupid."

Tamsin shrugged as a totally unintelligible loudspeaker announcement interrupted them. "Here, we'd better go in to see Shirley. What's the plan?"

"My mole," Feargal grinned, as he knew it always wound Tamsin up, "my mole tells me that they think Harry has his fingers in a few pies. He hangs around the Link with young lads - always a bad sign for someone well into his twenties. Mark, as we know, has a history of being drawn into crime, petty or otherwise, so there's a good chance they've gravitated towards each other."

"Poor Shirley does have a hard time with him. Right," Tamsin stood up. "Let's go and find her. This place is like a labyrinth, but I think it may be this way ..."

They located her after a few minutes wandering in wrong directions, following blue lines on the floor, then red ones. She was on her own, so Feargal was maybe right about Mark having legged it for the night. The patient wasn't overjoyed at seeing them, but with no way out she was sullen but prepared to answer their questions.

Tamsin kicked off. "I'm really sorry to see you here, Shirley. What's happening to Luke? Is Mark able to look after him?"

"Yes. Mark's a good boy." She gave a crooked smile and Tamsin laid a hand gently on hers for a moment. And Tamsin having broken the ice by talking about the two most important things in Shirley's life, the patient was surprisingly ready to tell them the whole story.

"I could see that Harry was no good. You get to recognise the type when .. well, after all these years I have a nose for them."

Tamsin nodded her understanding.

"So when I was driving to the supermarket and I saw him and Mark down the Link, heads together, looking as if they were up to something, I was shocked. I've tried so hard to keep Mark out of trouble!" Her voice rose in anguish and Tamsin touched her hand again, fearful of getting thrown out by some vigilant nurse.

"I know you have. You're a marvel, truly. Many mothers would just give up."

Shirley relaxed back onto her pillow again. "So the next day when I was passing the old bookshop and remembered Harry's office was above, I just went straight up. It was pretty stupid now I look back on it. But I'd do anything to keep Mark out of trouble," she looked appealingly at Tamsin. She'd barely glanced at Feargal.

"It's understandable," murmured Tamsin encouragingly.

"So there he was, the little rat, sitting behind his desk in his cheap suit. He was on the phone - probably scamming some poor person. I saw red. I cut off his call and ... oh I can't remember ... shouted at him to leave Mark alone. He looked so smug, and he laughed at me. That did it. I snatched up the nearest thing - some sort of letter-opener on his desk - and waved it at him as I shouted.

Then other people appeared and tried to stop me. I don't know. I just ran." She tried to pull herself up on her elbow, winced, and lay back again.

"I was running down the stairs. I must have still been holding the knife. And Harry caught up with me and grabbed me, and somehow - I got stabbed." She indicated her ribs. "I thought he'd hit me, so I carried on out to the street. And that's where I stopped and saw the blood. I think I fainted. I came to to find myself flat on the pavement, with all these people round me talking loudly. I banged my head when I went down - it's still quite sore." She raised the hand on her good side to touch the back of her head, and winced. "One nice person tried to keep me calm and said they'd called an ambulance."

"And Harry?"

"Nowhere to be seen."

Feargal spoke, "They're out looking for him. It shouldn't take too long to run him to ground."

Shirley muttered a very uncomplimentary word. "I've told Mark if he has anything to with him ever again ... I don't know what I'll do. He's actually pretty upset. He's been here most of the day. Maybe it'll sober him up. He's a good boy, really ..." She closed her eyes again.

Tamsin leant forward and took Shirley's hand again. "Let me know if you need any help with Luke. You need to rest now." Shirley nodded, her eyes still closed.

"I hope you're home soon, Shirley," added Feargal as he followed Tamsin out of the ward.

Chapter 20

While Shirley's injury didn't apparently have anything to do with the murder, it still made them all feel uncomfortable at the level of violence amongst the *dramatis personae*. So Feargal and Tamsin met at The Cake Stop the next morning for a powwow, and as Charity happened to be walking up the Hill with Muffin, she got roped in too.

"You always talk such sense, Charity," said Tamsin, as she settled them both in comfy armchairs with mugs in front of them, and Quiz and Muffin touched noses and renewed their acquaintance at floor level.

"I do try. And this whole situation seems awful. How's dear Emerald?"

"She's off on a yogic retreat. Best place for her. No phone contact and all that. So I hope she's cleansing her mind and washing her chakras or whatever it is they do. Not worrying about all this, anyway."

"Wouldn't it be lovely if we could solve it before she got back!"

"It sure would, but we seem to be stuck. Ah, here's the man himself ..." and Feargal came over to join them.

"Just having a chat with Jean-Philippe," he unloaded his tray onto the little table, which now bore three mugs and a plate with an enormous cheese and ham toastie. "Sorry - starving," he smiled as Tamsin looked daggers at his slender form, "Never keep still, that's my problem! Hi Quiz, hello Muffin," he added, reaching a hand out to each of them. They sniffed it appreciatively, then lay down beside each other again on Quiz's mat.

"And what did Jean-Philippe have to say?"

"He says one of the constables who'd been at the scene was here off-duty the other day having a coffee, and he got the impression that they were getting nowhere with the case."

"His impression is about right. Nowhere."

"Ok, let's look at what we have already," and Feargal took a big chomp out of his sandwich, chewed for a moment, then said, "We've got the ultra-suspicious Harry, who's a small-time crook, who's been hanging about with Mark and has accidentally -"

"*Maybe!*" interrupted Tamsin.

"*Maybe* accidentally stabbed Shirley and put her in hospital." Charity gasped and put a hand to her throat. "He's now on the run. He may be pushing drugs, and it seems he starts by getting the kids onto herbal smokes of some kind."

"So he may be in cahoots with Barry at the health shop," added Tamsin.

"He certainly drives a car that doesn't fit his income as a third-rate insurance salesman."

"How do you know he's third-rate?"

"If he were any good, old Prenderghast wouldn't have been so quick to sack him ..."

"Ahh, very true," Tamsin looked admiringly at Feargal. "But there's nothing beyond a threatening visit to the shop to connect him with Gabrielle."

"He seemed to be trying to rope her in somehow. So when she refused whatever it was he was offering, she clearly knew something about what he was doing. And he wanted her silenced?" Feargal took another crunchy bite of his sandwich.

"Sounds possible. And didn't you say young Cameron saw Harry go back up the stairs when the class was leaving?"

"You're right, Charity! How could I forget that?"

"And did you find a connection between Harry and the poor girl's brother?" asked Charity, popping a piece of crust from Feargal's plate into Muffin's mouth, "There you go Muffmuff." She looked at Quiz's big brown eyes, raised an eyebrow and picking up another piece of crust said, "May I?"

Tamsin nodded, "Ask her to do something for it."

Charity said "Look beautiful, Quiz!" Quiz, not knowing what these words meant, tilted her head most fetchingly. Charity smiled broadly and gave her the titbit, as Tamsin laughed, shaking her head.

"Nothing we can put a finger on," said Feargal. "Though it's possible Alphonse has an interest in doping horses in an undetectable way, and may be experimenting with herbs. It's been tried before."

"Alphonse appears to be the father of Saffron's baby," declared Tamsin. Charity looked suitably aghast. "And he's trying to weasel out of paying anything towards the baby's keep."

"Rat!" said Feargal, licking his fingers, while Charity frowned at this revelation, and snorted, "So he clearly has the morals of an alley-cat."

"And we don't know whether he genuinely liked his sister. She did visit him regularly."

"Perhaps she just liked horses. She was into nature .." said Tamsin.

"True. Inconclusive. Now what else have we?" Feargal sat back in his deep armchair.

"Kurt! Kurt was stalking Gabrielle and has in the past picked wild mushrooms, sliced them up, and presented them to her. Feargal and I will be trying to catch him this evening and find out when he last gave her some."

"That's so weird. Is he likely to own up to giving her some that Tuesday?" asked Charity.

"He's pretty thick," Feargal assured her, "Room temperature IQ."

"I guess you're meaning an American room?" quipped Tamsin. "If it were an English room it would be an IQ below 20, and that would be barely possible."

"Oh, you mean this new Centigrade thing?" Charity's face cleared. "I can't keep up with all these changes."

"It changed about sixty years ago!"

"There you go. A recent change!" Charity smiled beatifically as Tamsin and Feargal both smiled at their quirky friend.

"But I think he's sharper than we're giving him credit for," Tamsin returned to the matter in hand. "He holds down a job. And he certainly cares for his cat very well."

"And in your book, caring for his cat means he never harbours murderous thoughts?" Feargal teased. Tamsin turned her mouth down at the corners, and folded her arms in a theatrical gesture.

"If he was picking mushrooms for Gabrielle, it was presumably because he liked her. Why would he want to kill her?" Charity asked, reasonably.

"Obsessional?" Tamsin suggested. "Stalkers do end up killing their victims sometimes." She shrugged.

"So that's three possibilities you're looking at," Charity adjusted Muffin's position off her small lap which the little dog had crept onto, her paws digging uncomfortably into her mistress's thin legs, and onto the space beside her on the armchair. "Is that it?"

"I find it hard to think Linda or Andrew had anything to do with it. Nor Julia, for that matter. And it seems Saffron is fully occupied being a victim herself."

"There's Barry, Gabrielle's manager at the shop. If he was doing illicit stuff with Harry, and Gabrielle rumbled them ..."

"Harry's threats suggest that he was trying to get her to come in on his gig, and she wanted nothing to do with it."

"We need to look a bit more closely at Barry, I think." Feargal said, and they all nodded.

"It has to be someone who knew she was there. It was a dark night. There's no light showing at the back of the yard. It seems to be triggered by the café door opening."

"Makes sense, and of course at that time of night the café was closed." said Feargal. "I'll check that with Kylie in a mo."

"No stranger would have come in off the street, found her on the fire escape, and heaved her over." Tamsin sighed. "That narrows it right down.

We can actually place Harry and Kurt at the scene."

"And do you think it was two different people who killed her?" asked Charity.

"Got to be," chorused Feargal and Tamsin together.

It was later that day, after their inconclusive morning coffee chat, that the two intrepid 'detectives' found themselves lurking near Kurt's flat again.

Sure enough, his lumbering figure appeared out of the dark as he whistled tunelessly and jangled his door-keys.

"Hallo Kurt - we meet again!" Tamsin started breezily.

Kurt eyed them both up and down. "So you two's stepping out together, right?" he leered unattractively.

"Er, not exactly," Feargal said. "Just bumped into each other down the road."

Kurt started to advance to his door, and Tamsin quickly intercepted him.

"Thanks for telling me all about how to pick the right mushrooms, Kurt. Really helpful!" she nodded vigorously. "I think it's very sweet that you would prepare your finds for Gabrielle to put straight into her lunch. You must have really liked her."

"Arr. That I did." He shook his head sadly.

"So when did you last give her a surprise mushroom gift?"

Kurt frowned as he thought. "It'd be that last Tuesday, that would. Reckon I took some into the shop on Tuesday morning on my way to work. Yeah." He nodded slowly. "That were it. Tuesday."

Feargal and Tamsin glanced at each other, and Kurt suddenly took fright at what he'd said.

"But I didn't do her no harm! I didn't hurt her - I never! I ... I liked her," he mumbled, pushed roughly through them and in no time had disappeared into his house.

They walked on till they were out of earshot. "Well, well, well. That's one mystery solved," said Feargal.

"The question remains, *why?* Why would he give her deadly poison if he was soft on her?"

"Maybe a complete accident?"

"I dunno. He sounded pretty authoritative when he was telling me what to look for and what to avoid. Maybe he's one of those *savants*. You know, they can know loads of facts - to the point of obsession

- but can't understand people at all. He may be slow, but he realised he may have incriminated himself just now."

"But it's still not generally known that she would have died anyway," Feargal reminded her.

"You're right. Got it! He has to have given her Death Cap deliberately. If not he would have nothing to fear, as no-one knows about the poisoning. He wouldn't have reacted like that - all defensive."

"Looks as though we've found Murderer No.1."

"It does indeed. But we're going to have to talk to him again. Find out why on earth he did it."

"We'll have to corner him somehow so he can't escape this time."

"And I'm definitely not going into his flat again! We'll have to think of a suitable way to do this. And we haven't got long before Emerald's back."

"Sunday night? We have a lot to do!"

Chapter 21

The house seemed very empty without Emerald in it. But Opal had quickly transferred her affections to the new tin-opener and bowl-filler. She was at this moment on the window-sill catching a little cool Autumn sunshine while she set about her post-prandial ablutions, keeping her gorgeous long cream fur spotless.

And into this peaceful scene burst Tamsin and three eager dogs. Today Banjo was being asked to pick three beakers in the right order, so he could stack them inside each other. This game always reminded Tamsin of her grandmother's button box. Whenever she visited her grandparents, she made a bee-line for the middle drawer of the big dresser in the morning room of their rather grand home. It was a large old-fashioned tin with an embossed hinged lid, full of buttons of every shape and size. 'Waste not, want not' was one of Grandma's frequent dictums, having lived through the War, and no worn-out garment was ever discarded without its buttons being harvested and placed in the tin. Tamsin would play for ages, sorting the buttons into matching sets, or into size order, or by colours.

There was something very satisfying about sorting, she reflected now. And coaching Banjo into picking the right beaker that would slot neatly into the stack with a gratifying clunk, she could see that he found it just as absorbing.

It was time to introduce a fourth, smaller, cup, and at first Banjo grabbed the new "shiny object" and dropped it into the big cup. Tamsin waited to see what would happen next. Sure enough, when he tried to put in the next cup on top of it, it wouldn't fit!

She distracted him with a quick game with a toy for a moment, removed the new cup and encouraged her dog to get it right again with just the three beakers he'd mastered. "We always end with success!" she laughed as she collected all the beakers, released the other dogs from their beds from where they had been watching, and prepared to set out on a walk with the three of them.

And watching her dogs on the Common, snuffling, running, and exploring - according to their individual personality - she thought again about what Banjo had done.

While sorting the beakers to make them fit he'd been distracted by the new one and wanted it to fit next, without considering its size. Was this what she was doing in this case? Trying to force the evidence to fit her theory, grabbing the new information and forgetting what they'd learnt earlier?

Maybe this was why they weren't getting anywhere!

They knew now who had poisoned Gabrielle - but they were yet to uncover why. They had three other people who may have had reason to want her dead as well. What was she missing?

She thought of Shirley, still languishing in hospital from her stab-wound. She had seen this as a side-issue, a kind of sub-plot. But what if it weren't? Supposing it was central to the whole affair? She already knew quite a lot about the unfortunate Shirley, who'd spent so much of her life trying to keep her errant son on the straight and narrow, and she had no doubt that brandishing the paperknife had been merely an expression of her frustration and distress. She would never have used it to hurt anyone. But Harry? Would he be ready to injure anyone who went against him? How much did his drug habit affect his personality and his actions? Had he gone so far down the wrong route that he would take desperate measures to protect himself?

She texted Feargal. "Any news of Harry?" and quickly an answer pinged back: "Still no sign."

This was quickly followed by another message: "Talk later. I think I'm on to something."

She snapped her phone shut, wondering what it was Feargal was on to. And hoping that it was safe, whatever it was! And it was while she was tapping the phone to her lips thoughtfully, her dogs having run themselves out and now walking just behind her, that she recognised the lumbering figure of Kurt cutting across the Common ahead of her. She looked around quickly and noted the other figures - some with dogs, some without - scattered about the hill. She felt reassured and closed in on her quarry, slipping her hand in Banjo's collar as she approached.

"Hey Kurt! We keep crossing paths!" she said with enforced jollity.

"Arr, that we do Miss," he said, slowing down and halting in front of her. "These be your dogs?" and he reached out and patted Quiz clumsily on the head. The dog flinched, decided enough was enough and took up her station behind Tamsin again. Kurt tried to reach forward to Banjo, but a low grumble and a twitching of his lips sent him back again fast. "That one wicked?" he said crossly.

"Ah, he's not great with strangers, I'm afraid," Tamsin smiled and clipped the lead onto Banjo's harness. "Don't take it personally! How's your cat - Candy, isn't it?"

Kurt's frown evaporated and his whole demeanour relaxed as he talked fondly of his beautiful cat. Once they'd compared notes on Opal and Candy and he'd fully softened, Tamsin felt the time was right to drop in another mushroom question.

"Kurt, are you absolutely sure the mushrooms you gave Gabrielle that Tuesday were the right ones? Because she wasn't at all well that evening. I feel sure you know all about mushrooms and I can't imagine you'd make a mistake over something like that - especially as you really liked her."

Kurt's face crumpled and he took a few steps towards the nearby bench before sitting heavily on it and slumping forward. Tamsin perched at the other end of the bench and downed all the dogs so she could focus on what Kurt seemed about to say.

"I knew I done wrong," he began, then buried his face in his hands. There was a long pause.

"What did you do wrong, Kurt?" she said, quietly.

"I put in a different mushroom. A woodland mushroom, like."

After another long pause, Tamsin prompted, "Why did you do that?"

"It was only a little bit. Just one slice of the wrong'un in with the field mushrooms. She never noticed .."

"But why?"

"I wanted to save her. Be there for her when she needed me."

Tamsin's mouth fell open and she closed it again quickly. "Go on."

"I thought she'd just feel a little poorly, you know? Not bad. I only put in one little slice. I had a plan, see?" He turned his ashen face to her. "I was going to call on her after class. I knows where she lives. Lived. I was going to be there if she wasn't well. Make her feel better." He reached down to rip up a few blades of grass. Banjo tensed at his movement then settled again.

"So what went wrong?" Tamsin asked quietly.

"I went home to leave my yoga gear, and I set off again to go to her home. I'd noticed she felt a bit queasy during the session, and I thought here was my moment. She'd be pleased and she'd like me." He looked appealingly at Tamsin. "But as I walked past the back of The Cake Stop I saw her." He choked back a sob. "I saw her. There on the ground. She were dead. I could see that, plain as could be." He shredded the blade of grass angrily as he spoke, and Tamsin put her hand out to her dogs, glancing about and seeing there were still people about.

"I didn't know what to do. I panicked. You can see why? I thought I'd done a terrible thing and I panicked. I went straight back home and watched tv."

"You didn't think to ring an ambulance?"

"She were dead, I tell you."

Tamsin was appalled. This blundering bear of an imbecile had killed a lovely girl then gone home to watch television. Not quite yet had he killed her, it was true, but she'd have been dead by now anyway.

"How did she die, do you think?"

"Reckon she must have fell off that fire escape. I saw she went out there at the end of the session. I thought she were just leaving early."

"And why do you think she fell, Kurt?"

"I dunno, do I? Maybe she felt a bit queasy like and leant over the rail to throw up and ... and she leant too far."

"Ok, Kurt," she said after a moment. "Thanks for telling me. I'm sure you feel a bit better now, about her *accident*." Tamsin emphasised the word. She wanted to get away in one piece from this unpredictable man who seemed unable to see the outcome of his actions, or that he had any responsibility at all for what had happened.

"I do Miss, thank you. I'll be on my way now." And so saying, he smiled, stood up, brushed the flittered grass from his trousers, and strode off down the path.

And she made her own way shakily back to her home, put on an extra warm cardigan, cuddled all four animals, and was nursing a steaming mug of hot chocolate by the time she picked up the phone, dialled, and asked for Chief Inspector Hawkins.

Chapter 22

Tamsin felt bad shopping Kurt to the police. But really, she had no choice. Just because his perception was impaired didn't mean that he should get off scot free! The man was clearly a danger, even though he didn't realise what he'd done. She remembered Maggie telling her that just an ounce of Death Cap was enough to kill someone. And that's what Kurt had given Gabrielle. Just a few grams and her death warrant was signed. Even if she hadn't been attacked that evening, it would have been too late to save her. His ridiculous plan would have failed.

Tamsin shivered, and pulled her sleeves down over her hands. The only possible redeeming factor in the whole affair is that Gabrielle was spared the days of agony - by Murderer no.2. She gritted her teeth in a kind of impotent fury.

She felt sure now that Murderer no.2 had not been Kurt. A sudden eruption of barking interrupted her thoughts, and looking out of the window she could see Feargal's car pulling up outside in answer to her peremptory text summons. She went to get coffee ready and called "Come in!" as she heard his footsteps crunching down the gravel drive - and the dogs, recognising his step, stared intently at the gap between the door and its frame till the door opened and they were able to launch themselves at him.

"Am I glad to see you!" said Tamsin fervently as she brought the coffee to him at the kitchen table. And she told him the whole Kurt story.

"Wow. That's how they found out! I'd already heard they'd brought him in for questioning."

"They have? They won't be letting him out again, will they?"

"No chance. They'll have psych specialists all over him."

"Are you sure?" Tamsin peeled off her extra jumper, the fear beginning to ebb away. "Hey!" She started with alarm. "What about Candy?"

"Candy?"

"Yes, his cat! Oh Lord, I never thought of that. We have to ring them again."

"I'll just check he's in for the duration ..." and Feargal started rapidly tapping out a message. Then another. A frown, then another message.

"He's definitely not coming out before trial. The last thing they want is a potential serial killer on the loose, however loopy he may be."

"And Candy?"

"They've already sent the RSPCA round to collect her. Stop worrying. You did the right thing." He leaned forward and patted her hand avuncularly. "Now you're over that shock, get ready for another ..."

"More shocks? Wait, this needs reinforcement," and waving the empty cafetiere she went over to the kettle to do the needful. "Let's adjourn to the comfier chairs for this part of the story."

So they settled down, Tamsin on the sofa with her legs tucked under her and Moonbeam across her knees, Quiz sitting near Feargal's armchair with an expectant expression, and Banjo choosing to lie down on the hard floor right beside his expensive squashy dog-bed.

"I decided the time had come to talk to Alphonse," Feargal began. "So I rang him and said I was needing a quick interview about his life as an amateur jump jockey, and teased him a little by asking if he had any photos of him winning races, getting prizes and all that. He fell for it hook, line, and sinker!" He smiled smugly.

"So off I went to his grand horse hotel, and I got admitted into the house."

"Yeah? More than we were!"

"I could see evidence of another person. Not a casual visitor, I thought, but a resident."

"How?"

"There were two empty mugs, and a couple of empty plates with toast crumbs on the coffee table, and where I sat down on the sofa, the seat was still warm."

"Oh wow, Inspector Hawkins would be proud of you!"

"More than that, there was an overflowing ash-tray. Now athletes don't usually smoke, so I got out a pack of cigarettes,"

"You don't smoke!"

"Part of my reporter sleuthing kit," he beamed. "Tricks of the trade."

Tamsin smiled back and hugged Moonbeam to her.

"So I got out my pack of cigarettes and offered him one, saying 'May I?' very politely. And Alphonse says, 'No thanks, I don't.' So I apologised and put the fags away again, fortunately for me."

"So he has a smoking untidy house-guest."

"He does. And I'm pretty certain who it may be. There was also a suit jacket hanging over the back of a chair. A cheap jacket, like Shirley told us Harry wears."

"Cheap suit fits in with him, have to say …" Tamsin turned the corners of her mouth down. "But we need more than that, don't we, to know that Harry is that closely in cahoots with Alphonse?"

"We do. So when I left after doing the interview and getting copies of photos, I drove off till I found a turning that gave me access to the fields behind Alphonse's place. I always keep boots and a Barbour in the car, so I got into my walking kit and trekked across the field, keeping close to the hedge till I could see another barn behind the house. And what do you think I saw in that barn?"

"A boy-racer Merc."

"Exactly."

"That does look pretty conclusive, you're right. So should we tell Hawkins we've located his runaway? I don't think he'll be best pleased about that!"

"No-o-o. I don't think so. Yet." Feargal dipped his finger in the milky froth on his coffee and dotted the tip of Quiz's nose with it. They both smiled as they watched her going cross-eyed licking it off. "I think a visit to that shifty Barry at the health shop may be worthwhile."

"And it's half past two now! Let's go!"

Remembering that there was no "No Dogs" sign on the door of the health shop - something Tamsin habitually kept an eye out for and noted on her mental map of the world - they set off on foot across the Common, with Moonbeam in tow.

"I can always scoop her up if anyone objects," she said cheerily. She was glad to be doing something positive after feeling so bad for much of the day.

It was the day of the country market in Malvern, and they had to weave through the stalls of delicious produce to reach their destination. When they arrived at the shop, they found Rose at the till ringing up someone's purchases. As ever, she was looking totally bored, clearly doing the bare minimum required of her. Barry, on the other hand, was buttonholing another customer and giving them chapter and verse on where the product they were interested in was sourced, how natural and pure it was, and how it would cure everything from pimples to poxes …

"He's a real snake-oil type," Tamsin said quietly to Feargal as they feigned interest in a display of organic flours. "Wonder how he got into this business."

"Maybe he stumbled upon it in his search for making money. I sure get the impression that that's what drives him."

"Would fit. With Harry's sideline."

"Harry and Barry. What a double-act of shysters!"

"Watch out, here he comes."

Barry had run out of effusive sales-talk and his victim had slipped away to look at the dried fruit. "And how may I help you today?" he beamed, clapping his hands together. "That little dog won't do anything untoward I take it?" he asked, suddenly looking alarmed.

"Oh no, not at all!" And Tamsin lifted Moonbeam up and held her in her arms.

"You've been here before!" Barry suddenly recognised her, and frowned. "Asking after Gabrielle?"

"That's right! I was with my friend who was her yoga teacher. She's still *really* upset about this happening at her class, and as her friends, we just wanted to see if there's anything that can explain it."

Before Barry could deny any knowledge of anything at all, Feargal jumped in: "We're following up a lead." He gave a knowing man-to-man look at the shop-owner, who couldn't resist returning the look. Feargal looked about him shiftily and got closer to Barry. "Seems there's some guy who was annoying her. Name of Harry."

Barry started visibly. "Er, I think I know who you mean." He was clearly casting about for an answer. "She told me some guy had been in and pestered her. Yes, that's it! Harry."

"And where's Harry now?" Feargal gave him another knowing look.

"Uh, how should I know?"

"It was something to do with your herbs wasn't it? The herbs you're famous for?"

"Look, I run a clean shop here," he protested. "I can't help it if some ne'er-do-well tries to make something of what I sell. I don't know what you're suggesting. Here," he spied new visitors coming in, "I have to help these customers before Rose scares them away .." And he scurried off, composing his chubby features once more into an oily smile.

"You're getting heavy, Moonbeam. Let's go!" said Tamsin, and they gave a cheery wave to Rose who looked stonily at them as they squeezed past the new shoppers and left.

"Touched a nerve there, alright!" said a very pleased-looking Feargal as they emerged into the gloom of the October evening. "I think there's more to our Barry than meets the eye."

"He's shifty, alright. Here ... I've been thinking ..."

"Don't overdo it, girl!"

"Ha ha. I mean, what Cameron said. He said Harry went back up the stairs to the upper room to collect something that night, but then he left out of the front door with the rest of them."

"And?"

"I wonder if he'd have had time to run out to the fire escape, shove Gabrielle over the side, then come back down. What do you think?"

"I think that's a good thought - and we ought to check it out. Let's go over there now and experiment."

So they arrived at The Cake Stop and asked Jean-Philippe to unlock the Upper Room and did he mind if they made an experiment?

"If you can make *les flics* go away, sure!" he replied enthusiastically, adding *"Mais bonsoir, Mademoiselle* Moonbeam!"

"We're doing our best to restore the police to their traffic duties," smiled Feargal.

So first they unlocked the room and started from the top of the stairs. "You be Harry, and I'll shepherd this imaginary flock out of the front door."

"You'll have to go quite slowly. A mass of people don't go as fast as you would on your own."

"Good point. Now Cameron said he nearly missed his jump when Harry pushed back past him. Then, let me think … yes! .. that Harry caught up with them at the front door of the shop, outside. He must have caught up with them all before they even left the café, when Emerald locked the front door. Off we go." They started slowly down the stairs and when Feargal was almost at the bottom, he turned and ran quietly up the stairs again. Tamsin carried on walking slowly towards the front door, and imagined how long it would take to unlock it and herd everyone out on to the street. And Feargal was taking too long.

She'd been waiting a good minute before he came whizzing down the stairs again, narrowly missing Kylie and her tray of empties, and scooted out of the front door where Tamsin was waiting on the street.

"What took you so long?"

"I had to drop my yoga mat and towel on the floor, open the fire escape door, say some words to my imaginary victim and get her into the right position. Suppose she'd been sitting down? So then I gave an almighty shove to get her over the railings. I realised just a push wouldn't be enough. I would have to grab her and heave her legs over. Then I shut the fire escape door again, wiped my fingerprints off it, picked up my papers that I'd left on the floor on purpose, along with my yoga stuff, and hurried downstairs again. I think I actually came a bit too fast. Harry wouldn't have been rushing so obviously - just enough so he was catching up with everyone."

"So you don't think he can have pushed her over then?"

"Doesn't seem likely. Unless when he arrived she was in the right position and he simply flung her over."

"Either she'd have been sitting down feeling wretched, or standing up. And she'd have turned to face the sudden visitor."

"Agreed. I don't think he did it. Not then, anyway. I wonder where he went straight after Emerald locked up? He could have gone round once everyone had left."

"Good afternoon Tamsin! How nice to see you again!" said a soft voice. Tamsin and Feargal both started and turned to see who was addressing them.

Chapter 23

"Oh Damaris! How lovely to see you. Are you delivering another load of delicious cakes to Jean-Philippe?"

"I am!" The diminutive Damaris, the youngest and smallest of the Dodds sisters - also known as the Three Furies - who did the catering for The Cake Stop, patted her trolley which bore three containers of new cakes.

"Bit late in the day for you? I thought you normally did morning deliveries."

"It's been such a busy day. We had a special order from the new Italian restaurant on the top road. They've kept us busy all day. Though not as bad as the other week. They're new customers you see, so

Penelope is insistent we should do what we can for them to help get them started."

"Sounds wise," Feargal nodded.

"Anyway," she touched her hand to Tamsin's wrist, "it was gone 6 o'clock when they rang and said they urgently needed more gateaus. *6 o'clock!*" she added, archly.

Tamsin was fond of the Furies, so she was happy to oblige by listening to Damaris's tale of woe. "I suppose being new they underestimated their success. I've heard they do good food."

"I suppose that's the case. Anyway, if you'd come by here at 7.15 that night you'd have seen me trudging up the hill with this laden trolley. And that's when it happened."

"What happened?" Tamsin's ears pricked up.

"That man came rushing out of the alley just there. Nearly knocked me and all the cakes flying!"

"What man?" asked Feargal with some urgency.

"Well, I'm not sure. I couldn't really see. I was so concerned with rescuing my trolley and keeping it upright. But he did seem familiar to me. Does it matter?"

"It all depends which day this happened, Damaris."

"Oh, then let me think. It was just after they opened." She started counting on her fingers, looking into the middle distance. "They opened two weeks ago, and they're closed on Mondays. So it must have been Tuesday." She smiled up at them triumphantly, and her expression changed as she saw their faces.

"Tuesday two weeks ago? Then I'm afraid it matters very much," said Tamsin.

"And who it was matters enormously," Feargal leant towards the little baker. "Can you think, hard? What did you notice?"

Damaris screwed up her eyes and thought hard, as bidden. "About five foot nine, I'd say, not huge. But fairly broad. I think he may have had a round face, chubby cheeks you know …"

"Age?"

"Ooh, I'd say 30s, 40s? I'm really not that sure. Oh, I did notice one thing!" Tamsin and Feargal leant in towards her with bated breath. "He was wearing one of those beige overcoats - a trench coat, I think they call them? And it had a belt. It was undone, dangling. And the buckle flew up and hit me on the hand as we almost collided. That I can remember clearly because it hurt," she nodded eagerly. "Does that help?"

"It really does, Damaris, thanks! You may have just provided the missing link for us. You'd better get those cakes in to Kylie - in fact I think we should come in to sample them!"

Once more, Tamsin and Feargal found themselves seated in the comfy armchairs, Moonbeam on Tamsin's lap, enjoying coffee and sharing two slices of the new cakes.

"This is amazing!" said Tamsin as she licked her spoon.

"The cake?" asked Feargal.

"Oh that, yes, always. But I meant what Damaris saw. Who do you think it was?"

"Sounds to me like Barry. Five nine, forties, square."

"That trench coat should be easy to identify him. And when do you put a coat on?"

"When you're going home!"

"Exactly. How about we enjoy this coffee then mosey on over to the health shop around closing time. Let's see, it was 5.30 when Rose threw us out the other day. If we get there about quarter past and find somewhere out of sight to watch, we may just see Barry leaving."

"Good plan, Boy Wonder!" said Feargal. "Maybe we've had it wrong about Harry all along. Just because he's a rat,"

"And he's staying with an even bigger rat!"

"Maybe he has no ambition beyond being a rat. He doesn't aspire to anything as grand as murder."

"We need," Tamsin offered a few cake crumbs to a happy Moonbeam, "there you go, Bumbum - we need to find out why. Why would Barry want to kill Gabrielle?"

"And how did he know she was there?"

"That's simple. Got to be Harry. Harry must have told him. Maybe when he left the class Harry went over to meet up with Barry at the shop. It's only a few minutes away."

"Yes, that's all possible. But why? Why did Barry want his super-efficient assistant out of the way?"

"She must have been a real thorn in his flesh if he did it. Cos, yes, she was a great asset in the shop. Perhaps Rose was sent by the universe to pay him back for what he did!" Tamsin giggled. "No, I shouldn't laugh. It's so awful."

"And we have to nail whoever did it."

A while later they waved goodbye to Jean-Philippe and Kylie and started towards the health shop. The Friday food market had today given way to the Saturday craft market, which was still in full swing – and with the stallholders under their green and white striped awnings surreptitiously beginning to pack up their wares early, Tamsin and Feargal had no difficulty finding somewhere to lurk unseen. Tamsin couldn't resist buying a pretty beaded bracelet, while Feargal did his best to try all the cheese samples on the goats cheese stand and a few biscuit samples from the next stall as he kept watch on the shop door.

And it wasn't too long before their patience was rewarded. Out of the shop came Barry. He was threading his arms into his beige trench coat as he walked along the busy pavement, and they could see his undone belt swinging loose as he walked away.

"Guilty as charged," said Tamsin, picking Moonbeam up so she didn't get run over by a careless parent pushing a pushchair.

"Looks like he was definitely at the scene of the crime," agreed Feargal. "But was he there before or after .."

".. or during?"

"And was he in league with Harry?"

"Looks as though we have three very unpleasant suspects. At least poor old Kurt wasn't unpleasant, just dim."

"We need to check out their alibis."

"And their motives. That's the most important thing. Why would Harry or Barry want Gabrielle out of the way?"

"You know," said Feargal as they reached the top road and turned their steps toward the Common again, "I do think Alphonse is a slippery character who shirks his parental obligations, and who's maybe skating around the edge of illegal practices, but somehow I don't see him murdering his own sister."

"Hard to countenance, it's true."

"Let's clear our minds for a bit and see what we can channel!" and as they reached the edge of the Common, now darkening with a mystical dusk – the great Hills above them covered in swirling October mists – Tamsin unclipped Moonbeam's lead, and Feargal called out "Race you Moonbeam!" and set off down the grassy hill at a run. Moonbeam was delighted to accept the challenge and shot after him. Tamsin laughed as she watched her lanky friend, arms and legs flailing – he really is not very athletic, she thought – slow down and bend over to ruffle Moonbeam, who turned and ran back up the hill towards her grinning, tongue lolling.

"Off you go!" she cried, sending the little dog hurtling down the hill again. And by the time she caught up with them, she found Feargal sitting on the little stone bridge, his long legs dangling, and Moonbeam happily taking a cooling drink from the stream below.

It was a light, enchanting moment amidst all the stress.

Chapter 24

When Feargal had finally left on Saturday evening full of tomato and cheese pasta, they weren't very much further ahead. They'd narrowed it down to the three in the unholy alliance of Alphonse, Harry and Barry, but still didn't have anything solid to go on. It was all circumstantial.

Tamsin sighed and turned her mind to her *Top Dogs* work. She went through her messages as usual, and happily booked in three new clients. Then she listened to the last message.

"Ms Kernick? It's Chief Inspector Hawkins. I .. er .. I have to thank you for the information you passed on to us. It's helping us clear up a crime. But I want to make it clear to you that this investigation is ongoing, and I'd appreciate you keeping out of it.

I don't want you to be a "have-a-go hero" and give us another incident to clear up. Do you get it?"

"Golly!" Tamsin never liked to swear in front of her dogs for fear of offending their sensibilities. "He's cross! You'd think he'd be pleased with us, wouldn't you, guys?" The three dogs tilted their heads as they tried to detect any food-words in that sentence.

But later on she wondered what he feared. Another murder? The good but crusty Inspector must have considered there was still some danger.

And the next morning, the air clear after the rain and a weak October sun making the grass sparkle, she loaded the dogs into the van to take them up the Hills for a walk on Midsummer Hill. As she pulled out of Pippin Lane she totally missed the dark car that slid out from Bramley Drive and quietly followed her.

It was a beautiful day up on the Hills. The crisp October air invigorated her, and the wind - that had been absent down at house-level - was strong and gusty up here. She made sure to keep her little dog away from the edges of the steep inclines for fear she'd get blown over. And it was as she emerged from a clump of trees that she felt an arm gripping round her chest, and another hand tightly covering her mouth. Before she had time to think, Moonbeam grabbed the attacker's trouser-leg and shook it, growling loudly. Quiz jumped up and pushed him with her front paws, while Banjo barked ferociously and muzzle-punched him.

Remarkably, as Moonbeam started to tug and drag down his trousers, the man took one hand off Tamsin's mouth, so he could pull them up again. Tamsin screamed, he let go with his other arm and fled, tugging up his trousers as he ran, hotly followed by all three dogs and Tamsin, who took a moment to steady herself before chasing after them. That was when a runner hove into her view. It was Andrew! He was wearing his running kit and he was racing up the path towards where he'd heard the screaming and growling. Tamsin gasped "Stop him!" waving her arms furiously. And stop him he did.

By the time she caught up and told all the dogs to lie down, Andrew had the attacker firmly in his grip, one arm shoved up his back. "Ow! You're hurting my shoulder!" wailed the mugger.

"Alphonse!" Tamsin gaped at him. "What on earth ...?"

"I'm fed up with you poking your nose in. Wanted to - Ow! - warn you off."

With his free hand, Andrew - who was clearly much fitter and stronger than Tamsin had realised - waved his phone.

Tamsin nodded, still panting and a bit shaky, and he pressed the 9 button three times. As he spoke to the police, Tamsin took one of her rope leads from round her shoulders and carefully tied Alphonse's wrists together behind his back. Alphonse wilted and hung his head.

"What were you thinking? Were you going to kill me too?"

"Whaddya mean 'too'?" Alphonse said truculently.

"Your sister is dead, you may recall?"

"I had nothing to do with that."

"So who did?"

Alphonse hung his head again and didn't utter another word. In one swift move Andrew put him flat on the ground, face-down in the autumn leaves.

"Where did you learn that?" asked Tamsin, admiringly.

"Judo. Very handy moves," he grinned, keeping his knee lightly on Alphonse's back. But after a bit of squirming and complaining Alphonse didn't try and escape, and stayed still and completely silent while the police sirens wailed their way to the car park and two uniformed men arrived, tramping heavily through the wood.

"Want to press charges, Miss?" asked one, while the other replaced Quiz's lead with handcuffs.

Tamsin lifted her chin. "Yes. Yes, I do. I'm fed up with bullies in this case. And if it hadn't been for my brave dogs," she indicated the three dogs, still lying down where she'd asked them to, "I don't know what may have happened. Yes. I most definitely do." She folded her arms and flashed an angry look at Alphonse, but he was still staring sullenly at the ground, so she filled the police in with his name and address and they led him away to their Panda car.

Once they were gone, she put a hand to her head. "I feel a bit funny," she said and sat heavily on the grass, swiftly approached by her dogs who reckoned she needed more help and that licking her face was the way to go to restore her equilibrium.

"Here, you need to recover. Delayed shock," said Andrew, who sounded as if he knew what he was talking about. "Our house is just down this path. Put your arm round my shoulder .." And so saying he helped her to her feet and the two of them walked unsteadily down Midsummer Hill to Andrew's home, followed by the three dogs.

As they came in the front door, down the short flight of steps from the road, Andrew called out to Linda, who came through the house from the back, shedding her gardening gloves as she came.

"Goodness! What's happened? You look awful, dear. It's Tamsin, isn't it? Emerald's friend?"

"She's been attacked up on the Hills - no, don't worry!" said Andrew as Linda's face fell. "The miscreant is in police custody now. But Tamsin's had a shock."

Tamsin found her legs had suddenly gone wobblier and was grateful to find herself laid out on the sofa facing the huge picture window with the vista of the Welsh mountains in the distance, glimmering in the sunlight. Quiz and Banjo lay down on guard in front of the sofa, while Moonbeam hopped up and lay beside her, as Linda draped a warm throw over both of them.

They brought her tea and sweet biscuits, and generally fussed over her till she felt better.

"Can that one see alright?" asked Andrew, nodding his head towards the grey and white Banjo.

"Why do you think he can't?"

"One of his eyes is light blue. Thought it may mean something."

"Ah, gotcher. It goes with his blue merle colouring - some have two blue eyes. I love his blue eye!"

"So do I," said Linda. "I think he's beautiful."

Tamsin relaxed and leant back, closing her eyes.

Having heard most of the story from Andrew while Tamsin dozed, Linda turned to her so she could fill her in on what had happened just before Andrew had arrived.

"What a horrid man!" she exclaimed. "What a mad thing to do!"

"I'm not sure any of that crowd are operating with a full deck," said Tamsin. She was feeling a lot better now and had swung her legs to the floor and was sitting with the blanket round her shoulders as she sipped her tea and munched her biscuit, Moonbeam on her lap dealing efficiently with any errant crumbs. "I think they may all be on something or another, and it's impairing their judgment."

"Well, that's a very polite way of putting it!" said Andrew.

"And no excuse whatever!" added Linda, archly.

"Look - thank you so much for rescuing me, Andrew - it was fortuitous you came at that moment. One of the reasons I love that walk is because it's normally so quiet!"

Andrew smiled back at her, "Happy to have arrived at the right moment!"

"And thank you both for giving me time to recover. I really appreciate it." Tamsin stood and reached for her dog leads, but lurched and grabbed the sofa arm.

"Here - you're still a bit wobbly. Let me drive you to your car. Do you think you'll be able to drive?"

"Thank you - I think that's a good idea. I know Alphonse is in custody now, but ... you know?" She tried to suppress a shudder, unsuccessfully.

So Tamsin squashed into Andrew's sports car, Moonbeam on her lap and the two collies jammed between her knees. Andrew took her to the car park where they could see a large dark car parked next to her van. Tamsin pointed to a badge on the windscreen giving admission to Cheltenham Racecourse. "Must be Alphonse's car. The rat! Hope he's got a pile of parking tickets when he comes back to get it."

"Maybe it'll get towed," said Andrew hopefully. Then he continued his knight-in-shining-armour role and ensured Tamsin was sensible and able enough to get her van out of the car park and on her way before leaving her. He followed her till she was clearly comfortable on the zigzag bends, then gave a cheery toot-toot as he peeled off.

And as soon as Tamsin got home she rang Feargal.

"I already heard! They're questioning the rat now. You ok?"

"Yes thanks. I wasn't. But I was nursed and loved by Linda and Andrew, and I feel much better. I was able to drive back home."

"Linda and Andrew?"

"Two of Emerald's folk. Nice ones."

"Well that makes a pleasant change!"

"Most of them are nice! It was Andrew who showed up at the right moment, trapped the rat and made the citizen's arrest. Do you think we've got them all now?"

"I do not! The police have Kurt and Alphonse. But all three of that crowd need to be locked up one way or another. They are miserable people and they egg each other on in their nastiness. Got to be stopped."

"Time to tell Hawkins about Harry? And get him to round up Barry too?"

"I think so."

"He's not going to be pleased! He rang to warn me off last night. But there I was, walking my dogs, minding my own business ..."

"Well, I'm glad you're ok. Emerald's back tonight isn't she? You won't be alone?"

"Yes - it'll be lovely to have her calm presence here again. And I have my lovely dogs too - they were brilliant! Wish I'd had it on video - Moonbeam stopped him by pulling his trousers down!"

"That would be hilarious if it weren't so serious ... Tell you what - you put your feet up and watch tv for the rest of the day. Really. Shock is a funny thing. You can always ring Charity to sit with you if you feel wobbly again. I'll get the info to Hawkins' people. They'll just have to deal with the fact that we've solved it and they haven't!"

"But we haven't solved it!" Tamsin wailed, her hand pressed to her head.

"The police will grill Alphonse and get whatever they can out of him," said Feargal, his confidence shining through his words. "With the knowledge that he's harbouring Harry who's on the run after putting Shirley in hospital, they'll have a lot to work with. They'll know where to pick Harry up. And while the evidence round Barry having killed Gabrielle is circumstantial, it's pretty damning. They'll want to question Damaris, of course - get her statement."

"None of them seems to be very bright. And they're so weaselly. I guess it won't be hard with proper police interrogation techniques to set them against each other and break them down."

"True. That's where the professionals shine. think you should feel very proud of yourself, Tamsin! And Emerald's going to be so pleased," he added, with warmth in his voice, "to know that it's all over."

Chapter 25

Tamsin took Feargal's advice and spent the afternoon lying on the sofa covered with cat, dogs, and a warm blanket, zoning out on old movies to distract her from all the recent goings-on.

And by 6 o'clock she felt very much better. She cast the blanket aside, lifted Opal up above her at arm's length and swung her gently to the floor, and got up. With a big stretch she picked up from the floor her mug and bowl and three chocolate bar wrappers (where on earth had those come from?) before heading to the back door to put all the animals out for a few moments. Then she started casting about the kitchen for something to welcome Emerald home. A quick poke around in the fridge gave her some ideas, and she settled on lemon pancakes and asparagus.

"Some people would think that a strange combination," she confided to her four-footed audience, who could recognise food preparation when they saw it, and were paying rapt attention. "But I think it's perfect!"

And so, by the time Emerald arrived home around eight, the animals were all fed, the pancake mixture was ready and the table laid. Tamsin had found some bright red rosehips lurking out of sight in the damp garden, and had put them in a pretty blue jug on the table.

Emerald got the full canine greeting, as well as much cuddles and purring from Opal who saw her usual tin-opener back again, and a big hug from Tamsin.

"You're glowing!" she said as she studied her friend's face. "Good weekend?"

"Brilliant! Just marvellous. I feel amazing. Three whole days of yoga and meditation." Emerald's face fell. "If only I didn't have to come back to this awful thing hanging over me .."

"Not another word - I have news! But first of all, let's eat. Opal's in need of another cuddle, I think - she's been weaving round your ankles while the dogs mobbed you." She set about cooking their meal.

"Hey, you're good at tossing those pancakes!" laughed Emerald, sitting at the table with Opal purring on her lap.

"Sadly for the dogs, I am. Look at them - all living in hope that I'l drop one," and she looked at the three dogs lurking near her, Quiz and Moonbeam sitting alert watching her, and Banjo lying behind them, his dappled grey head turned away, chin on paws.

It was after everyone had settled down, they'd polished off the pancakes and had adjourned to the living room with mugs of coffee, that Emerald said anxiously, "That was lovely! Ok, so what's this news?"

"It's all over! Well, all over bar the shouting."

"Ohh! That's wonderful news!" Emerald clasped her hands together expectantly.

And Tamsin set about telling her the whole story of what had been happening in her absence. About Shirley and Harry and old Prenderghast; about Saffron's baby, the herbs-to-drugs racket, the horse connection, Alphonse's involvement, Kurt's horrifying confession, and the Furies' damning evidence against Barry. And she ended up with the attack on herself, and how Andrew had come up trumps.

"So," she finished up, "it was all nothing to do with you, and it will all be forgotten again soon enough."

"Harry! And that man from the health shop! And Gabrielle's *own brother!* I can hardly believe it. It's true that Harry was always a bit of a queer fish, no good at yoga at all. And he only started coming recently. And as for Kurt … oh dear oh dear. What a very sad thing. I knew he was a few *asanas* short of a practice," she grinned for a moment, "but I had no idea he was that batty. Do you think he realises what he did?"

"I haven't heard. Probably not. 'Simple' is a polite way of putting it. Doubtless he'll be attended by shrinks of every sort. Hopefully they'll be able to let him out at some time - I dunno how that all works."

"Not sure he should be let out, with judgment that impaired. But what about his cat?" Emerald looked alarmed as she remembered the long-haired cream cat so like Opal.

"It's ok. The RSPCA collected her as soon as they wheeled Kurt in. They've probably found her a new home already - she's so pretty. The thing is, it's all over! And while two of your students fell by the wayside, a few of them came up trumps! Shirley the crusading mother should be home soon, and Saffron will be able to get her rightful support for her child. Linda and Andrew were brilliant. Cameron's keen eyes gave us plenty of clues. And it was Sara who put us on to the horsey connection with those herbs."

"What an amazing group of people I've managed to collect!"

"Too true! And I'm proud to say some of them are in my collection too. You know what? I'm really looking forward to getting back to normal, when the most exciting thing that happens is turning a corner with a wayward dog, or finding the Furies have created a new cake ..."

"You and your cakes!" laughed Emerald. "But I know what you mean. Just getting back to the even tenor of our days ..."

"Where on earth did that phrase come from?" Tamsin interrupted.

"Dunno! Some poem or other we had to learn at school. I'm probably misquoting it horribly. Anyway, I'll be glad to find the most exciting thing of the week is Saffron at last being able to do the splits."

"Ouch! She's only just had a baby!"

"She is pretty supple, though, and she's been working on it."

"It seems such a long time since all this kicked off. And hey, I've been thinking this afternoon while I was watching old black and white films - now this is over I can go back to planning the walk I was talking about a couple of weeks back. Remember?"

"I do! You mentioned it that day we first found the mushrooms. When my feet got soaked," Emerald smiled, and stretched her wiggling toes out to the fire.

"That seems so long ago ... I'm not sure I'll be eating mushrooms again any time soon," Tamsin said ruefully. "But back to the walk. A-a-a-nd, I thought - how about making it a Dog and Yoga walk? Your people are all fit and would surely enjoy a hike over the Hills - I think it could be fun! And you may pick up some more students from the doggy crowd. What do you think?"

"That's a brilliant idea! You may get more students out of my people too. You did well last time, I seem to remember. Gave your classes quite a boost. When will we hold it?" and they fell to pulling out their calendars and spent a long time happily planning a route, designing the flyers, deciding who should ask Feargal to get it announced in the *Malvern Mercury*, who should invite who, and all the rest of the things they had to get in place to make a howling success of this event.

"And this time there will be NO disasters!" said Tamsin when they were done, as she put aside the plans and leant back in her armchair with a sigh, automatically fondling the ears of the dog whose head happened to be in her lap.

Chapter 26

Tuesday afternoon saw the friends gather at The Cake Stop again. But this time they were meeting well before Emerald's students were due to arrive. Tamsin hurried in from the print shop with a package of flyers for the Big Dog Walk. She already had it open and was giving Kylie a handful to display when she spotted Feargal and Emerald over at the window table, and she waved happily to them. They each sat on an armchair, and had put their coats on the one they were saving for her. Today Tamsin had Quiz with her, and she dropped the lead and sent the dog over to greet her friends, while she ordered her coffee.

And they hadn't been seated round the table long before another dog came wiggling across to join them - it was Muffin. "You don't mind, do you? I invited Charity along."

"Of course not," laughed Feargal, "though, knowing Charity, she probably knows all about it already!"

They pulled up another chair, got everyone sorted - "Come along Muffymuffs, sit on my lap," said Charity - and Feargal began.

"I have heard .."

"Tssst!" chorused Tamsin and Emerald.

"What's that, dear?" Charity looked puzzled as both Quiz and Muffin tilted their heads to try and discern what the noise was.

"Tssst! It's the noise moles make," the two women giggled.

"Ha ha." Feargal feigned grumpiness, and grinned. "Anyway - I've heard ... news of the miserable threesome. Seriously - listen up."

They all composed themselves and listened attentively.

"As we know, these three were all in the drug racket together. Harry was already dependent, and a pusher, and he'd roped Barry in by using his herbs as a gateway drug with the youngsters."

"Evil!" tutted Charity.

"Too right. Barry got in touch with Alphonse via Gabrielle - "

"I thought it was odd that he had his phone number!" interrupted Tamsin.

"And of course he wanted to take it much further and make a mint from hidden horse-doping. So there was a lot of money at stake, and when Gabrielle - who'd rumbled what they were doing - seemed in danger of spilling the beans, they decided to act. Alphonse insists he never meant her to die - just be warned off, but he claims Barry took it too far."

"Thieves fall out!" said Emerald.

"And snitch on each other to save their own skins," added Tamsin.

"It was a pretty tenuous link at the best of times - they're all amoral self-servers. So Harry was on the run after lancing Shirley. It seems her Mark was being recruited to push on the street, and she rumbled this and wasn't having it. Harry was over at Alphonse's place and told him what a pain you were being, Tamsin. So he decided to warn you off."

"And what a mess he made of that!" Tamsin snorted.

"What happened, dear?" Charity turned to stare at her.

"Don't worry, I'm ok. I'll tell you in a minute: my brave dogs saved me! Let's hear the rest of this sad story."

"That's about it, really. They each denied touching Gabrielle, but both Harry and Alphonse were quick to point the finger at Barry. And along with Damaris's evidence, it was 'fingers' that finally clinched it." Feargal leant forward and spoke quietly, "Barry's fat little hands exactly match the handprint on Gabrielle's ankle. It was like he signed his name on his victim."

"Eek!" "Ooh!" "Yuk!" the three women all said at once.

"Once he was faced with that evidence he completely broke down. So they're all going for trial. No bail. Two for assault, one for murder, and all of them for conspiring to pervert the course of justice. Looks like we'll be rid of them for a good while."

"And I imagine Alphonse will have to look for a new career when he comes out," said Tamsin. "The

Jockey Club's pretty hot on this kind of thing, isn't it? Wonder where that leaves Saffron and her child support?"

"It seems he has quite a bit salted away in various companies. The tax people are like terriers once they get going on tax fraud. It'll all be uncovered, don't you worry. And he'll lose more than his trousers this time!"

There was a silence as they digested all this information. And then Jean-Philippe, who'd been perched on a stool just beside Feargal and had been listening to the whole thing, spoke up, "Tamsin the Malvern Hills Detective strikes *encore!*" he beamed. "I'm so glad this awful thing is over! I have a lot to thank you for. Coffee on the house for all of you - and what *gateaux* would you like?"

So by the time Emerald's students began to arrive, they were relaxed, well-fed, and feeling at peace with the world. As the *yogi* all came in, they pulled over another table and added chairs as needed. Feargal and Charity were introduced - though everyone seemed to know her one way or another already - along with Quiz, who Cameron was delighted to see again after the escapades in the Nether Trotley case.

It had been decided to keep the details of the news to themselves, but Emerald did make a little speech, once they were all settled.

"I'm really sorry for what we've all been through over the last two weeks. I know you've all been questioned, as have we. But it seems that the police have got the culprits ... and Harry won't be joining us any more."

There was much murmuring, some head-nods, a couple of "did-you-ever's" and a "I always thought he was shady .."

Emerald went on, "Let's have a moment's silence to remember Gabrielle." And for a short while they became still and bowed their heads - all except for Cameron who was having a silent eyebrow-raising conversation with Quiz.

Then Emerald said, in a more matter-of-fact voice, "I'm afraid I don't have any more details to give you, but I'm sure the *Malvern Mercury* will have it all once it becomes public knowledge." And she sat down again.

Tamsin jumped up and held up her flyers. "Look, we're going to blow all this out of our minds with a windy walk up on the Malverns, and you're all invited! It'll be such fun! Who'd be able to put out some flyers?" and they all became enthusiastic, asking for a wadge of flyers each.

As they settled again, Linda, looking about, saying, "I see Shirley isn't here? Is she ok?"

"Shirley met with an accident last week - but she's ok! - and I hope she'll be back for a light practice very soon," Emerald explained, and before anyone could ask more, Cameron piped up, "Kurt's not in his usual place by the stairs," pointing to the empty space.

"You're too observant for your own good, young man!" laughed Feargal. "Kurt won't be here either. It seems … it seems he misunderstood something, and he's getting some psychiatric help."

Cameron opened his mouth, but before he could come out with an inappropriate schoolboy remark about being bats in the belfry, Molly said loudly, "How's your hot chocolate Cameron?" and closed the subject very effectively.

Jane and Alice, for all their faults, knew when some twittering would be useful, and both jumped in with mention of a happening in one of their favourite soap operas, and as they steered the conversation away, the party started to chat amongst themselves.

Tamsin took the opportunity to thank Linda and especially Andrew. "Think nothing of it," he responded gallantly, and jumped to his feet as the door opened and admitted Julia and Sara. His face lit up as he found chairs for them and offered to get their drinks, eager to tell them the latest.

Tamsin smiled at Emerald as she saw she noticed, and whispered, "It seems as if a romance is blossoming here?"

"Judging by Andrew's attentions, and Sara's pink cheeks ... you could be right!"

"They're well suited - outdoorsy types, both of them."

Tamsin leant back in her armchair and surveyed the throng of friends, now relaxed as they chattered, and looking forward to their yoga practice. It had been a horrid event, but three bad people were now under lock and key. She sighed, and Feargal turned to her.

"Enjoying the fruits of your labours?" he asked.

"It's as it should be. People happy and getting on with each other. We're all different, but these people - look at them - they're all doing their best, and being kind to each other."

She put a hand down and touched Quiz's head as she watched Cameron kneeling beside Charity, stroking Muffin.

"Kindness is what it's all about," she smiled, as Feargal turned to watch Emerald.

Chapter 27

It was a beautiful bright but chilly Sunday morning a couple of weeks later, and a long procession of people and dogs trailed up towards the Worcestershire Beacon, with Tamsin and her three dogs at the front, Emerald more or less in the middle, and Feargal at the back, chatting to Andrew who'd volunteered to help steward. This offer had been gratefully received, as walking up the Hills was challenge enough for Tamsin, never mind running up and down them, the length of her crocodile!

Before they started, Tamsin issued some brief instructions. "There are sheep about, and steep drops. I know many of you have well-behaved dogs, but as there are so many of us here today, I'd like us to keep them all on lead for the entire walk." Many heads nodded sagely. "Of course when you're up here on your own, you can have your dog off-lead - as long as you know you can call him back fast! Let's spread out a bit, so we're not all on top of each other." And after she'd said a few more words on how to manage the younger dogs in the group and a firm reminder about clearing up after their dogs, they all began to set off.

As they climbed, Tamsin admired the magnificent views all around them. The Herefordshire Beacon with its Iron Age earthworks at British Camp rose up behind them. Out to the left the clear air showed the Black Mountains of Wales a shimmering pale blue, with the patchwork of fields and woodland laid out in the fertile valley below them. To the right they looked over the several Malvern towns and villages - Great Malvern, Malvern Link, Malvern Wells, Little Malvern - and the Cathedral City of Worcester, the mighty River Severn sparkling in the Autumn sunlight, and beyond towards Warwickshire and Oxfordshire.

"Which county are we in?" asked Cameron, who'd run up with Alex, five-year-old Joe struggling to catch up.

"The Hills are actually in three counties," replied Tamsin, who loved showing off her local knowledge. "Do you know what they are?"

"Worcestershire!" shouted Cameron.

"Herefordshire!" shouted Alex.

"Yorkshire!" shouted Joe, and ducked beneath the onslaught of abuse and withering looks from his big brothers.

"Well done boys. The third one is Gloucestershire. But do you know how many counties can be seen from the top of this hill?" She pointed to the outcrop of rock on the path up ahead of them.

"Five?" suggested Alex.

"Twenty-five?" Cameron tried.

"Two hundred!" shouted Joe triumphantly before turning and running back down to his parents and baby sister.

"It's between your two suggestions," smiled Tamsin. "You can actually see fourteen counties on a good day. But please don't ask me what they all are!"

As the boys scampered back down to find their family and their dog Buster, Tamsin felt the smile broaden on her face, and her shoulders relaxed as she enjoyed the wonderful landscape of her chosen home.

"You've got a great turn-out again, my dear," puffed Charity as she caught Tamsin up - greatly helped by Muffin's enthusiasm to see her friend Moonbeam. For once Charity let her dog haul her along, thankful for the help.

"It's amazing! People are so good," said Tamsin, turning to look back fondly at the long column of people following her.

"Not at all - it's you who's good to organise it. Everyone's happy to have the opportunity. They love meeting other dog-owners who they know won't do anything nasty to their dog. And if they've learnt with *Top Dogs*, that's definitely true!"

"And I see that Emerald's got loads of her yoga students here, from all her different classes. Didn't realise she had quite so many. I heard her the other night talking to Penelope - you know, of The Furies - and she may be doing a private class for the three of them in their home."

"What a good idea - I imagine baking in a hot kitchen all day is very physically demanding. And I doubt they have time to get to any classes - they're so busy with their catering business."

"I'm just hoping she gets paid in *cake!*" Tamsin grinned as she looked down the long straggling column of walkers and saw Andrew, who had been patrolling up and down beside it, Suddenly he spotted Julia and her Schnauzer Romeo along with her two children, and homed in on Sara and Grouse.

"Tamsin!" It was Maggie, closing in on her with Jez the black Labrador.

"I see Tamsin the Malvern Hills Detective has been hard at work again," smiled Maggie. "I really should be more careful what I say ..."

"Ooh, you never said a thing!" laughed Tamsin, as Maggie's husband Don, who was also a doctor, smiled like an inscrutable Cheshire Cat.

"Well, I'm glad you gave old Hawkins a run for his money. He's bustling around the station telling anyone who'll listen how good his team was to bring in such a haul of criminals. He's hoping no-one remembers how you get there ahead of him!"

"He should be glad. It's helping his clean-up rate."

"All brownie points for him leading up to his retirement."

"I hope he isn't replaced by some super-efficient whizkid!" laughed Tamsin. "I've just about got the measure of this Chief Inspector."

By the time they arrived at the peak, the crowd growing and milling around the rocks, pointing out their own homes and villages in the vista below, there was plenty of custom at the toposcope - the brass disc mounted on a granite plinth which identified everything you could see from the Beacon.

"Now you can work out what those fourteen counties are, Cameron," she smiled as the boys heaved themselves up to get a good look at the labels, pointing and chattering as they found names they recognised.

At last everyone arrived at the top. Tamsin moved about chatting to her students, and introducing herself to Emerald's yoga people, mostly identifiable by virtue of having no dog. Andrew had found Sara to walk with, with her father's very happy and over-excited Labrador Grouse who was loving all the attention.

"Yes, that's a great idea," Sara was saying, "my mare Crystal will be back in the holidays. Let's borrow another horse and go for a ride!"

Tamsin smiled as they passed her, then spotted Feargal who had caught up with Emerald and were just climbing up the hill. They make a handsome pair, she said to herself and to Quiz, who was also gazing at them as they reached Tamsin.

"Great turnout of your folk, Emerald!"

"And yours!" she replied. "I've had a few enquiries already from some of your dog people. Seems they've all been chatting together. How about you?"

"Same here! I was just talking to those two girls over there. One of them has a puppy she's struggling with, and her friend wants advice on choosing a dog."

"Ah yes, Mandy loves that puppy - I had suggested you already, really I had! - but this walk has obviously sold her on the idea."

"Looks like it's a handy marketing exercise for you both," said Feargal.

"True. But mainly it's fun. Isn't it glorious up here? I love it."

"It feels a million miles away from murder and nastiness ..." agreed Emerald.

"Yes, it's quite the opposite. Look over there - people are sharing their food that they brought with them," and she nodded towards the boulder-strewn space just beyond the Beacon, where people were sitting on the rocks, opening flasks and offering hot drinks and snacks to each other. "Isn't that Shirley over there - I'm amazed she's recovered enough to make this walk already!"

"She has Mark dancing attendance on her. I noticed he was being very solicitous as they climbed the steeper stretches," said Feargal.

"So he should be!" both women said at once.

"Tamsin, I'm loving this!" said Julia, as Romeo surged forward to greet his trainer. "Before I met you, Romeo would never have been able to manage all these dogs and people."

"You've put in the hard yards, Julia - it's down to your work."

Julia blushed. "I seem to have lost my companion," and she winked as she nodded her head in the direction of Sara, now in deep conversation with Andrew. "It's nice that they get on, though. And I met Saffron here," and at that moment Saffron, the sleeping baby Charlie strapped to her front in a baby-carrier, caught up with them.

Saffron was out of breath, Fuzzy Bear in one hand, and Napoleon's lead in the other. "Goodness, Charlie's getting heavy!"

"Napoleon managing ok?" asked Tamsin.

"He started off with lots of yapping, but I stayed at the back. I think he's worn out now."

"Perhaps he's finding that people aren't so bad! I saw Maggie giving him some treats. Here Napoleon," she said as she delved in her treat bag and gave him a sprat, which he wolfed down then sat attentively, wondering if another was on offer. "If you can organise a babysitter, you'd enjoy classes, Saffron. It'd be good before young Charlie gets the legs under him."

"That would be great. I think I'd like that. And I want to thank you for getting through my baby-brain and sending me off for advice - you know, for support for Charlie. I can't believe Alphonse did all those dreadful things." The time for subterfuge seemed to be over as Saffron spoke his name. "I kept quiet about who he was because I was ashamed of having been cast aside. Such an old story ... Now I'm going to keep quiet because I'm ashamed of who I managed to choose to be my baby's father."

"I don't expect you were looking at it like that at the time?"

Saffron blushed. "Course not! But I'm different now, now I have Charlie to look after. And I don't really want him to know too much about his father."

"Who knows, he may change. While he's cooling his heels at His Majesty's pleasure, he may have time to reflect. And I suppose with him being in jail it'll take time to sort out the support. But I believe the taxman has got his claws into him? Anyhow, you'll be able to get on with your design business again soon, won't you."

"Yes - I'm really looking forward to it now." She put her hand on her sleeping baby's downy head, smoothing down the black wispy hair. "I've been buried in nappies long enough - time to look ahead! And I can tell you, Tamsin, as soon as I've got any money coming in I'll be booking Napoleon into one of your classes. Your dogs are amazing!"

"That will be great! I'll look forward to that. And I'm sure that you having outside activities will make Charlie's world all the richer." And as Tamsin passed Napoleon another sprat, she said, "I hear you are to be congratulated!" as Linda - graceful as ever - walked over to join them.

"Oh, doesn't news travel fast!" laughed Linda.

Saffron looked puzzled and said, "What news?"

"Linda's looking to take over the health shop!"

"Amazing!"

"Thought I'd grab the chance. I'll be able to take it over as is - except I will certainly be cutting down on the exotic herb section!" laughed Linda. "I'm going to modernise the design, open up the café area a bit more, so we can hold talks there."

"Sounds terrific! Do you get to take over the delightful Rosie too?" Tamsin grinned.

"She's ok. Just needs a few rough edges smoothed over. She's actually been very reliable through all this upheaval. Turned up for work with no idea whether she'd be paid."

"Bet she's glad she still has a job?" asked Saffron, then added, "you know, until my own business gets busy again, might you have some hours available for me? You know design's my thing?" And Tamsin left them discussing employment as she drew away from the crowd and gazed down at her three special companions, who'd been waiting quietly during all the chitchat.

"We're going to go on a lovely long walk together tomorrow, guys, just you and me." They all looked at her expectantly. "You'll be free to run and sniff and chase and ... be dogs!"

"Talking to yourself, Tamsin?" said Feargal, drawing up beside her, Emerald close behind him.

"I'm addressing the three most important people in my life!" she corrected him.

"They're lovely - your dogs are a perfect advertisement for *Top Dogs*! You're getting known for your dog walks, Tamsin," said Emerald.

"Better than being known as The Malvern Hills Detective," she smiled, as they all laughed in the fresh November sun, which was already dipping towards the tops of the mountains.

Ready to read the next book in this popular series? You'll find **Barks, Bikes, and Bodies!** *here:*

https://mybook.to/BarksBikesBodiesLargeP

To find out how Tamsin arrived in Malvern and began Top Dogs, you can read this free novella "Where it all began" at

https://urlgeni.us/Lucyemblemcozy

and we'll be able to let you know when Tamsin's next adventure is ready for you!

And if you enjoyed this book, I'd love it if you could whiz over to where you bought it at https://mybook. to/DownDogLargePrint *and leave a brief review, so others may find it and enjoy it as well!*

All the Tamsin Kernick Cozy English Mysteries in Large Print

Where it all began ..

https://urlgeni.us/Lucyemblemcozy

Sit, Stay, Murder!

https://mybook.to/SitStayMurderLargeP

Ready, Aim, Woof!

https://mybook.to/ReadyAimWoofLargeP

Down Dog!

https://mybook.to/DownDogLargePrint

Barks, Bikes, and Bodies!

https://mybook.to/BarksBikesBodiesLargeP

Ma-ah, Ma-ah, Murder!

https://mybook.to/MaahMaahMurderLP

Snapped and Framed!

https://mybook.to/SnappedFramedLargeP

Christmas Carols and Canine Capers: A Howling Good Christmas Mystery

https://mybook.to/ChristmasCozyLargeP

Game, Set, and Catch!

https://mybook.to/GameSetCatch

All of them!

https://mybook.to/TamsinKernickCozies

About the Author

From an early age I loved animals. From doing "showjumping" in the back garden with Simon, the long-suffering family pet - many years before Dog Agility was invented - I worked in the creative arts till I came back to my first love and qualified as a dog trainer.

Working for years with thousands of dogs and their colourful owners - from every walk of life - I found that their fancies and foibles, their doings and their undoings, served to inspire this series of cozy mysteries.

While the varying characters weave their way through the books, some becoming established personnel in the stories, the stars of the show are the animals!

They don't have human powers. They don't need to. They have plenty of powers of their own, which need only patience and kindness to bring out and enjoy with them.

If you enjoyed this story, I would LOVE it if you could hop over to where you purchased your book and leave a brief review!

Lucy Emblem

 facebook.com/lucyemblemcozies

Printed in Great Britain
by Amazon

60493196R00157